The

Novus

By Lincoln Hartlaub

ISBN (Paperback): 979-8-9865307-0-3
ISBN (eBook): 979-8-9865307-1-0
For permissions visit:
www.LincolnHartlaub.com

Table of Contents

Chapter 1

WE SIT IN silence as the pot of water boils. The burner is half broken, and often turns off. Amica walks to the stove, lifts the lid, and sighs as she realizes it still hasn't boiled, "No luck," she mutters, "ever."

The hunger within me rattles louder as she says this.

I sigh too, and she sits back down. Staring at the table, a single lock of hair falls to my eye, and I brush it away before saying, "I'm not sure if I'll be able to stay much longer. I have to go home and study."

She glares at me with her silver eyes—the ones that strike fear into anybody's soul—and says, "Alice, you've been studying for six years."

"Yet I still feel unprepared." I say.

She assures me that I'll do fine on the test, but I'm not completely sure. She tells me I'm a clever person, but clever people are the ones who think they have it all together, only for everything to fall apart.

We wait a few more moments before we hear the fizz of bubbles rising. Amica releases a smile and lifts the lid quickly. My stomach stirs, and I feel the saliva building inside my mouth as she pours the dried noodles into the pot.

The hunger inside me makes me dread the wait. I attempt to distract myself by focusing on the details. The golden noodles make a crackling sound as they're dropped into the bubbly water. The bubbles begin to calm, and it reaches a harsh simmer.

I haven't eaten since yesterday. The government only gives us so much food in a week, and last week they didn't give us enough. I'm not sure about Amica's situation, but from her dull stare at the water, I assume she's the same way.

"Now would be a good time for one of those instant cookers." She murmurs.

They are quite nice but a luxury like that is out of the question for students like us. We can hardly afford textbooks.

Instead of saying that, I just nod. The noodles cook, and Amica occasionally stirs while talking about tomorrow, "But how can we be sure that the test isn't fake? I mean, the test could really just be separating rich and poor."

My gaze switches from the water to her eyes. She seems content with her speculation.

I frequently worry about Amica's choice of words. If she were to talk about this in public, she would be arrested immediately. The law of our city allows free speech but only so far as our President will allow.

If you were to speak against Pura City, he would find some way to eliminate you in secret. President Atrox wants people to love the city, and any negativity could cost you dearly.

She continues speaking freely, saying every thought that comes to her mind. The only reassurance of her safety is that she has good self-control. I trust her to not expose her thoughts in front of others.

"How can they get away with enslaving people?"

I cut her off before she says anymore, "Amica, you've said it before. Trust me, I know."

I exhale, feeling as though I was too harsh. I hope I'm not; this friendship can't die, it's the only one I've got.

There is less than five minutes left for the noodles when the power goes out. Thankfully, it's daytime so I can still see. The oven goes off, and the water stops boiling almost immediately. My stomach groans at the thought of not eating. Again.

I stutter before saying, "I'll just go."

Amica nods, and I make my way downstairs. Her house is very similar to mine since almost all student housing is the same.

On my way out, I'm greeted by Amica's mother, who is wielding her signature robe. She always wears a purple robe, along with excessive makeup. She puts so much effort into her face, yet never leaves the house. She tends to have Amica run errands.

I can't blame her. She's been through a lot. Everybody has. During the war, her husband died in a bomber plane. Not that she liked him. Anybody who worked as a bomber was usually despised. I suppose that doing her makeup gives her a self-indulgent way to cope with her loss.

I wave and exit through the door. My student housing is less than a two-minute walk away. Not everybody needs student housing, but since Amica's mom doesn't work, she gets it. I've lived in student housing since my mother died two years after the war ended.

She died of an unrecognizable disease. I never saw her corpse because the disease was contagious, and I certainly couldn't plan a funeral. After all, I have no money, and the city ruled the death *non-significant*.

It made me angry to think that they could decide whose life was important. My mother volunteered in the refugee camps and helped distribute food to the tents. She may not have been a public figure, or a government official, but she was important to those who knew her. So why should those who didn't know her rule her life *non-significant*?

My father died seven years ago, during the war. I was never close with him, but it still felt as though I lost a part of my life.

Ever since then, I moved out of my mother's house, and into student housing. I kept the same house-slave I had before, Tabitha. She was a criminal before the war, a bank robber. It's hard to believe that since she's so kind. I guess that was her cover.

Like Tabitha, all the criminals became slaves after the Purification. The government found it impractical and a waste of space to make prisons. So, they made all criminals slaves to the city. The only new slaves are the people who score low on the test. As Amica would say, it's unfair to fail one test and be considered a criminal.

On my way home, I stop at the grocery store, where I get my weekly food rations with my city student card. I swipe the card, the machine beeps, and the cashier gives me the student package. The cashier typically ignores me, and I appreciate it. I prefer not to talk too much, and she respects my boundaries.

Today, I notice that in the student package there are a few ready-made sandwiches, and some fresh fruit.

I exit the store, finish the short walk home, and then walk up the staircase that leads to the top floor of my house. I move my finger to a small black box by the side of the door, and it scans my fingerprint. The door opens shortly after.

I walk through the narrow doorway, and into the foyer. The government-issued student housing is supposed to look modern; everything is a bright white and dark gray. And yet, most of the houses aren't taken care of very nicely. The white walls are covered in grime, and the furniture is ripped in some spots. I try to clean, but between going to school, and studying for the test, my time is booked.

I'm disappointed to see such beautiful homes go to waste. The downstairs is only two rooms. The kitchen is small and covered with dust. The living room is packed with furniture, and the wooden floor has stains.

I try to imagine a time when it looked better. When the walls were shiny, and the furniture was nice.

I begin to walk upstairs to my room, when Tabitha bursts through the kitchen door. I try to run upstairs faster—to avoid her—but she stops me in my tracks.

"Alice! You know better than to run away from me!" She says this in a deep and powerful voice.

I walk back down the stairs, annoyed, because I don't really want to talk to anybody. I just want to study.

"Hello, Tabitha." I mutter.

She wastes no time, "The pipe under the sink is leaking again."

"Then handle it yourself. I have to study." I snap. I didn't intend to snap, but it came out that way.

She groans before releasing me and I run up the stairs quickly.

The hallway is short, and the ceilings are low. Only two rooms branch off. One is the bathroom, and the other is my bedroom.

When I walk in, I'm not surprised. Tabitha still hasn't cleaned. The gray blanket is tearing, and the pillow is unevenly stuffed.

As I sit down in my desk, the table wobbles because one of the caps have broken off. I erase the thought from my mind and focus. I need to pass this test.

My backpack is stuffed underneath the table, folded away with piles of textbooks. I slide it out of the tight gap and rest it next to my chair. Only now do I notice that the back of my chair is breaking as well.

I unzip the backpack and slip out a thin laptop. It's interesting how they get smaller every year but get more expensive at the same time. It isn't good news for students. I feel foolish for buying a decorative case, and a city seal sticker when I got some money a few years ago. The case is a light blue, and the city sticker is the Pura flower. A classic symbol of peace. It has a few petals, and the flower itself is white. I don't support the city, but everybody seemed to be getting one at the time. I wonder how I could have been so ignorant.

Before I open the laptop, I search my backpack for a random textbook. It's a small game I've created, where I pull out a random textbook and study the contents. It keeps me occupied for a while.

The one I choose is a two-inch thick hardcover book. It's titled *The Magna Council: A comprehensive guide to the elite forces.*

It's an excellent textbook, almost all students own a copy. While the Magna Council is typically despised, almost everybody takes an interest in it. I am guilty as well. I just so happen to pull out this textbook almost every time.

Despite me reading it over and over, I don't want to be on the Magna Council. Almost nobody wants to. These people are forced to stay in a room within the government building, making decisions for the city for an entire year. The thought makes my lip quiver. The few people who want to be on the Magna Council are megalomaniacs.

Everybody wonders how they make it seem so alluring. Nobody wants it, yet everybody is intrigued.

The Magna is made up of the people who scored the highest on the test. I think I'll score high enough to be an average citizen, and the government will give me just enough money to live in the city. If I score too low, then I will become a slave.

It's become a strategy for people to not try too hard. People don't want to be on the Magna Council, and they don't want to be a slave. They attempt to manage their score, but it's difficult. You don't know the number of questions, or the weight of each question. Without this information, it leaves people guessing. I've given up on this strategy. I don't want to risk it all.

My thoughts drift deeper into contemplation. I've thought about if the test is worth it many times. I remember before the test, when you were innocent until proven guilty. Now, the government assumes whoever scores low on the test is guilty. But what if Amica is right, and the test is fake? There are many conspiracy theories about it, and I'm not sure which ones to believe.

The only thing I'm sure about anymore, is that things need to change. The good can't be evil. And if we assume that they are, then the evil will grow. And if the evil grows, then there will be no good left.

Chapter 2

I REMEMBER WHEN the war ended. We all celebrated the end of evil and called it the Purification. I celebrated too. We hadn't known about the test yet, and we were just excited that the war was over. No more bombs, no more refugee camps, and no more death.

Except, there was more death. I remember very clearly. At the Purification, the entire city gathered in the city circle. Prince Atrox was tied to a pillar, and President Atrox stood in front of him. I knew he would be executed, but I didn't know what would follow. A deep realization. As the president pulled the trigger, I knew that evil was still present. There will be more war. More death. Evil will never dissipate.

11

Prince's eyes seemed to lose all depth, and I knew that he was dead. Prince Atrox was no more, and President Atrox smirked at the crowd. It made me sick to watch him kill his own brother with a smile. But neither of them were good. They both bombed the world and killed millions of innocent people.

It was at that moment, when my mother hugged me. Her arms wrapped around my shoulders, before she leaned in close and whispered, "It's alright. The good always wins."

The crowd cheered in the background of her faint voice. They cheered for the death of an enemy. She planted a kiss on the top of my head, and I knew that my mother was wrong. That everybody was wrong. The good won't always beat the evil, because there's hardly any good left.

After this, the president announced the test. All hope for the future died. People wanted to scream, and protest, but they didn't know enough. Yet. They didn't know that almost everybody in the first year would fail.

Many tried to escape the city. They thought they had better chances of surviving in the wild. But they couldn't leave. Once you're in Pura, you can't get out. Even if you could, you wouldn't survive. The nearest colony is miles away, and they don't tell us where because they want to keep us trapped. Control is their greatest weapon.

12

Pura accepts stragglers from the outer colonies, but they're forced to take the test if they're over eighteen.

Until you're eighteen, the city gives us housing, slaves, and free school. In return, we are forced to take this test. The city expects that eventually everybody will pass the test, and we'll be a perfect society.

It all sounds like a great idea. To eliminate all people who are likely to cause problems in the world, to prevent another war. To take a test that separates people who are likely to be criminals, from average citizens. However, I think that the failed students shouldn't be put in this position. The Purification was only six years ago. The first-year people hardly got a chance to study.

I think about all of this while I'm studying. I've moved onto the next textbook named *How to Treat a Slave: The Official Guide.*

It's my least favorite textbook. The methods they provide are disturbing, and almost nobody uses them, except for the government. The slaves in the Pura building are treated the worst.

I get a strange sensation within my stomach telling me to stop studying. If I keep going, then I might confuse myself more. It's been six years. *I must be ready by now.*

It's tempting to keep going, but I must rest. Not that I will. It's the night before a life changing test.

I do my best to set the untidy bed and lie down shortly after. My body shifts uncomfortably throughout the mattress, and I can't seem to get comfortable.

The entire night, I lie thinking about everything. The springs in my mattress, the hard pillow, but mostly the test tomorrow. I do everything I can to distract myself from it. At one point, I heard somebody walking around. Probably just Tabitha.

It's these boring thoughts that help me fall asleep.

My eyes begin twitching, and I awaken to shuffling feet outside my door. *Tabitha.*

As I bring myself to get up, my body quickly resists. Is it worth getting up? I lie there, contemplating if I should. If I failed to show up, then I would become a slave.

Right as I get up, Tabitha sprints into the room screaming, "Alice! You know better than to sleep past your alarm! Especially today."

I groan and drag myself from the bed. She exits the room, and I go straight downstairs. Her yell bellows through the house, "Breakfast is ready!"

As she screams, I think about my neighbors. Their slave doesn't need to wake them up because Tabitha probably does. She's different from the other slaves. Even though she's required to serve me, she does it with joy. She doesn't seem to mind the city's horrible system.

I arrive in the kitchen, where a charred muffin sits on a plate next to a scrambled egg. As I get closer, the smell grows worse, and so does the look. The egg is barely cooked.

I gulp it down anyways and run upstairs. The plan is to leave in an hour, and I still have to get dressed. It's customary to dress nicely for test day. Although it's not required, people would look down upon you if you didn't. It's very difficult to make it happen though, because most students can't afford elegant clothes.

The most I could afford was a smooth blue dress, along with a knock-off golden bracelet. I also found a necklace with Pura's flower. It drapes around my neck and flows onto the blue dress. The golden bracelet is a simple circle that encapsulates my wrist.

The dress was on clearance in a discount store, and I also got a student discount. It couldn't possibly get any cheaper.

I pull my hair into a tight, neat bun, and secure it with a band. When I'm done, I look neat and tidy. My brown hair is sleek, and the dress seems sophisticated.

A satisfied smile spreads across my face, and I think to myself, *I'm ready.*

I run through the house and out the door before Tabitha can embrace me for another awkward encounter. The door slams shut behind me.

The school is only a few blocks away, and I can see its highest point from here. About halfway, I glance around the street to see if I can find Amica. She might already be there.

Along the side of the street, are many tight, and compact buildings. Some are student housing; others are normal homes or offices. Most are abandoned due to the growing wealth in the city. This is bad news for Amica and I, but there's nothing we can do. Once Pura City formed, the rich instantly owned almost every industry, leaving no room for anybody else.

I walk past my old house and can't help but remember my mother. Every time I walk by it, I think back to the past six years when Pura City was formed.

At only thirteen years old, everybody else was still being a kid. I was the only one studying. It seemed like I was the only one who feared becoming a slave. Even Amica was putting it off. So, I began obsessing over the test.

My mother would walk into my room to find me studying. She would have to pry the textbooks from my hands just to get me to eat dinner. I knew that I couldn't become a slave. No matter how much I studied, I felt I needed to study more.

It was during this time when Amica and I began to grow apart. She was disappointed that I never wanted to do anything. My answer was always, *let's study*. Her face displayed so much sorrow, and I tried to do the same. But I couldn't. I couldn't bring myself to do anything else. My mind was corrupted by the test, and I couldn't bear the thought of failing.

Failing makes you a slave, is what I told Amica. Everybody knew that, but they didn't seem to care. It eventually got to the point where I would cry whilst studying. Tears would begin to flow, and I wished that Amica would be here with me. *Study. Please.*

All these thoughts made her stay away from me. She could tell I was agonizing over the test. My obsession was ruining everything. So, I stopped. I forced myself to stop studying excessively. I promised myself that I would stop only until Amica began to study.

Slowly, I returned to my normal self. Amica and I were friends once again, and I apologized to her. She insisted that she shouldn't have ignored me. She knows she should study, but she told me she's waiting for the right time.

I didn't know when the right time would be, but a tiny voice nudged my mind. It was pleading for me to study again, but I waited anyways.

I'm finally at the first of three buildings to the school. They are all connected by large glass corridors that branch into classrooms. I wish this building was mine, but it's only the elementary sector. The university section is on the opposite side.

I continue the walk but stop as I notice a loose line forming. Hundreds of university students line up on their way to signing in. I join the line at the end and stand silently. Most people are on their phones, or slurping coffee. I have no phone, and can't stand coffee, so I wait.

The line moves at a steady pace, and I see soldiers enclosing the students. They stand fiercely in their dark blue uniforms, each one embroidered with Pura's flower on their shoulder. Their helmets are gleaming, and their uniforms are lined with gold. I wonder if they'll attack us but realize they're just here to make sure nobody runs. *Control.*

The thought makes me wonder how many people attempt to run away from Pura, and how many succeed. They'd certainly never tell us, and we'd never find out.

"Next." I'm nearing the front of the line already, and I'm surprised by the efficiency.

I can now peer into the lobby, so I search for Amica. I can't see her, but she might already be in her classroom.

The lady perched behind the desk is not the usual secretary, but instead a young woman in her soldier uniform, "Next."

My daze is broken, and I walk forward slowly. Her face displays an irritated look, and I go faster.

The Novus

"Press all five fingers of your right hand onto this pad right here." She gestures towards a small black box on the desk and waits for me.

I raise my hand to it, and make sure to press down all five fingers.

"Please apply more pressure and turn your fingers to pick up the entire print."

I do as she says, and a few seconds later, her computer beeps. She stares at the screen, and then at me, before saying, "All right, that's you," She squints at the screen for a second before continuing, "Alice Kingston. Go straight to your classroom."

I nod, leave the desk, and make my way through the complex. As I walk, I look in every direction to see if I can find Amica anywhere, but I don't see her. She has to be in her class by now.

There are six senior classes this year, and Amica and I are in different ones. I arrive at the entrance of my classroom. The door is a huge frame of glass at least two times taller than me. Each classroom has glass walls, ceiling, and some of them even have glass floor. Not mine though. Mine has a rough gray carpet.

I walk to my desk, which is placed near the back of the classroom. My teacher, Dr. Ashton, has already perched herself at her desk, waiting to start the test. We still have time before we begin, so I make myself comfortable. I set my bag behind my chair and slide out some of my books. I skim

19

through them but feel restless. I decide to get up and grab a textbook from the classroom library.

As I approach the shelf, I peak through the glass wall and notice Amica in her classroom. But something feels off. She's wearing a blue shirt, with gray jeans. It's a strange choice for test day. I vaguely remember helping her pick out a dress. It was dark blue, and she picked it out a week after I got mine. She paid using her student city card alongside six coupons.

She sits quietly, observing her desk. She just stares at it, for no apparent reason. No textbooks or computers lay before her. Only the desk, and her thumbs. Around her, people run frantically grabbing textbooks, and studying intensely.

Study. Please.

But she doesn't. She sits silently, content with absolutely nothing. I tap on the glass—trying to get her attention—but I'm silenced by my teacher. I'm devastated but know that I must walk away. All I can do is hope that Amica pulls herself together enough to pass this test.

I sit back down and observe other people doing the same. I realize that Dr. Ashton has placed herself at the front of the classroom, where she is going over the tutorial. *Listen.* But I can't, I can only hope that Amica is listening.

"This is the most important test you'll ever take. It doesn't just determine your level of smarts, but your role in society."

The Novus

We already know this, but they still review it every year.

"The low scoring students are considered criminals. The high scoring students are considered superior, intelligent, and kind. There have been exceptions to this, but only a few."

She continues explaining, and eventually gets to the format of the test. We will be doing a standard multiple-choice test, short answers, and two written essay portions.

"You all are given the option to take the test on paper or computer this year. When making the decision, consider your typing speed, versus your writing speed."

Even before today, I knew that I would choose computer. I type faster than I write. Most of the class chooses computer as well.

"When you take this test, you will ignore your foolish desires of failing, not paying attention, and not making effort. You need full focus to achieve maximum results, and keep in mind that everybody is capable of being on the Magna Council."

She talked for just a few more minutes. It was a thirty-minute introduction, and she begins passing out computers and papers.

When I receive my computer, I immediately open it. We aren't allowed to start yet, and the computer is stuck on a white screen.

Dr. Ashton collects herself and sits back down at her desk. She pauses for a moment—while staring us down—before finishing with, "You may begin."

Our screens light up with a small green button in the center. It says *begin*.

Chapter 3

AN ANIMATION PLAYS across the screen like a rolling wave, before displaying the first question. I feel a knot grow in my stomach and I wish that I could untie it.

Explain the roles of our society.

It seems easy enough, so I type without hesitation. My fingers fly across the keyboard, typing every word that comes to mind. It feels natural as I type this answer. This is what we're trained for.

Pura City is divided by a Role-Placement Test, which sorts you into one of three categories. The first category comes from the lowest scoring percentile, which results in your enslavement. Slaves serve for life, working in homes, sanitation, or the Pura building. They have no rights.

23

The second category grants you citizenship in the city along with a job. This could be anything from running a store, to teaching students, to an entry-level government position. The job (and the job's income) are based on your test score as well.

The third category is for students who score above average, giving them a place on the Magna Council. The Magna Council oversees city decisions and leads the city completely. They are only overruled by the President.

It's been only three minutes when I finish the short response. The paragraph looks clean, and the words seem to flow.

As I move on to the next question, I notice a small timer pop up in the lower corner. *Six hours.*

Sweat begins to form on my temple, and the knot within my stomach tightens. I can feel loops tying at a rapid pace. My jaw clenches, and I realize that I need to keep going.

I go through each question slowly. The first portion of the test is about the concept of our city. The three roles, economics, and living conditions.

The questions become more challenging, and I'm relieved when the screen switches to portion two. It's titled, *History of Pura.*

This section talks all about the history of the city, along with the war. It's made to test our ability to retain information.

Most of the questions ask about the war, and our personal experience. Mine was good and bad.

I met Amica during the war but lost my father. I lived in refugee camps and survived a few bombs.

I find the responses challenging to write. I pause many times, being careful to take deep breaths. I force myself not to cry, and not think about the experience. Just. Write. That's it. All I have to do is write the response and move to the next question. But I'm wrong. For at least fifteen questions after that, I had to talk about the war. About my experience, and every single detail. I can't recall the exact moment when tears began to fill my eyes. But they did. A lot of them came, and they didn't stop. I see Dr. Ashton eyeing me from her desk, but she takes no action.

I finally finish this section after over two hours. It was decided that this year we won't have any breaks, so, I grit my teeth and keep going.

The final section of the test is the longest. And the most difficult. It talks about how to live in our society. It's titled, *Response.*

I take a deep breath and click begin. I'm stunned by the first question:

How would you react to your master shocking you with an electric current?

Pura doesn't openly share what happens to the slaves. Most people assume they're just put in specific houses and forced to work. Most are directed to the Pura building, and those are the unlucky ones. They are treated poorly and become rather thin over time. While Pura doesn't broadcast their horrible treatments, it's assumed.

I crank out answers to each question, trying not to get attached to any specific one. Most of the tears have stopped at this point, because I'm no longer sad. I'm angry. Angry that they treat people this way.

I glance towards Dr. Ashton who still watches me from her desk. She glares at me while yelling, "You all have fifty minutes left."

I worry for a few seconds but know that I must keep going.

The final question is an essay, and I find it difficult to write. The question irritates me the whole time:

How would you treat a slave?

It appeared simple to me at first, but every word I write makes me question the response. Obviously, I can't write what I would like to. The answer is supposed to be brutal. But I can't do it. You can't hide from the system.

I attempt to manipulate the answer, but it doesn't work good enough. Nothing does.

I jump as Dr. Ashton announces, "Ten minutes!"

My body shudders at the thought. Ten minutes left to determine my future. I write the essay slowly, still being careful to finish on time.

The Novus

When she calls out five minutes left, I conclude the essay. After reading it a few more times, I breathe. It's out of my hands now.

At the bottom corner of the screen is a button that reads, *Complete Test.*

The cursor hovers over the button, and my mind races as I contemplate whether I should click it. I attempt to get my breathing under control, but it only accelerates. The button taunts me, as though it's poking me in my neck trying to irritate me. I manage to produce one normal breath and click the button. *Done.*

The screen goes black, and I close the computer. I find myself squeezing my knuckles. As they turn white, all the thoughts come flooding. *What did I get? Did I finish too early? How did Amica do?*

The questions begin to settle because I realize that I must be patient.

Five minutes pass, and Dr. Ashton finally yells, "Times up!" Screams of terror bellow throughout the classroom, each one coming from a student who knows they've failed.

Computer screens go dark, and Dr. Ashton immediately begins collecting papers.

"Anybody who works even a second past the deadline becomes a slave." She threatens.

I try to glance through the glass wall to find Amica, but instead find that they've drawn the blinds on the other side. After Dr. Ashton finishes collecting papers, she puts the computers onto a cart. As she walks back to her desk, she looks at us silently.

"You all are dismissed for lunch. You will get a free period the rest of the day, and then gather in Purgatio Hall when the scores are ready."

Everybody immediately leaves.

Chapter 4

I RUSH OUT of the classroom, following everybody else. When I make it to the hallway, people are crying in their classrooms, and even more in the halls. Students sit on the ground, sobbing. I can tell who finished and who didn't.

I try to keep myself together and make my way to the lunchroom. I pause for a moment to see if I can find Amica in the hallway but come up empty. I assume that she's already in the cafeteria, so I make my way there.

The walk to the cafeteria is short, and I get there in less than a minute. When I walk in, I'm greeted by the usual loud noises of the lunchroom. Usually it's loud, but today it's exceptionally loud.

I walk up to the lunch line and am quickly filed to the front. The lunch lady gives me my tray, and instead of thanking her, I rush around the cafeteria searching for Amica. It would be nice if we were sectioned into strict groups, but instead I now have to look everywhere.

While glancing at a nearby table, I notice Amica on the other end. I don't walk over right away, because I notice that she's sitting alone. Amica usually has a crowd around her.

But Amica sits silently, staring at her food.

I slide into the seat across from her and try to act normal. It's extremely difficult considering we just took a life changing test.

Her eyes stay directed towards the table, and I risk a slight glance. She must have noticed, because her silver eyes meet mine. Although, they're no longer silver. They're gray. It's as though any feeling has been drained from them. I dread what she's about to say.

"I know I did horrible." She says, solemnly.

My eyes avert from hers, and I can tell that she senses my unrest, "I'm sure that you did fine."

She begins chuckling sarcastically while shaking her head. I don't blame her. Why would my simple reassurance lighten her mood?

We just poke our food. I notice other people doing the same. Nobody has an appetite, although I do notice one girl walking around the lunchroom. She carries on as though nothing happened.

The sight is disgusting. I find myself wishing for her to be a slave. I know that's wrong.

I manage to eat a few bites of food, and coax Amica into doing the same. The lunches aren't fantastic, and they hardly satiate us. It's funny how we were starving yesterday but don't have an appetite today. It feels wasteful.

Around us, students crowd around each other asking how everybody did. It's interesting how you could almost tell how everybody did. The people who are alone didn't do very well, and the ones who crowd around each other probably scored average. It's too difficult to tell who got on the Magna though. It's such a small minority.

This pattern goes on for another two hours, before the professors walk into the lunchroom. At the sight, everybody goes silent at once. We all stare at them, and they return our gaze before saying, "Everybody is to file into Purgatio Hall. There, we will announce the scores."

I gulp, nervously. Already? Is that good or bad? Did everybody do good, so it was easy to grade, or was it all bad, so they went through it quickly. I'm not sure they've ever told us how long it takes to grade.

I bite my lip, as everybody makes their way to the single file line. I lose Amica in the crowd, and notice that she's a few people back.

We finally reach the exit of the cafeteria and follow the line down the hallway. I walk down the hall, up some stairs, and then through another hallway. We arrive at Purgatio Hall, and slide through the big glass doors slowly.

Usually, the hall is more of an auditorium with a stage, and big red curtains. Today, the seats have been removed and the curtains have been removed as well.

The dim black walls are decorated with a gray trim cascading down the side. This is the only room in the building that isn't covered in glass.

The stage has remained intact, and they are already sorting people into their groups.

"Zeek Tenor, Ziw—" yells a professor over the noise. All the professors are running down a similar list, and I worry that I'll miss my name.

I search for Amica, who was behind me, but now has disappeared, "Where are you?" I mutter under my breath.

I continue searching and thinking until I hear Dr. Ashton call, "Alice Kingston." I freeze. What was she calling my name for?

I begin to pace towards her, and she finally says, "Get in line with the Magna Council."

A grin crosses her face as she says this, and it crossed mine too. I make a beeline for Dr. Ashton, and I scream with relief and joy until I see Amica on stage with the new group of slaves.

Chapter 5

MY SMILE SUBDUES, and I feel myself fall to the floor. It's embarrassing, but I don't care. The screams, and shouts that come from the hall are all silenced within my mind. It all blurs together, and my thoughts scatter.

Amica can't be a slave, no way.

A voice shatters the blur of my thoughts, and I finally hear it, "Alice, are you all right?"

The professor attempts to help me up, but I push her away and lift myself, "Yeah, I must have lost my footing."

She glares at me, and I can tell that she can sense the trickle of doubt in my voice. She guides me to stand in a line with five other people. It's a larger Magna team this year, usually only three people are chosen.

One of the professors waves a dismissive hand, and the new Magna Council begins moving, "You all will go up to the balcony."

She leaves us there, and we walk up a steep staircase. When I reach the top, I can see Amica sitting near the edge of the stage. The slaves have already been grouped into sections, but I can't tell which is which. I can only hope she's a house slave.

The new Magna Council walks to the railing and leans upon it since there are no seats. The view is incredible, and I can easily see many students illuminated by the beaming lights. It's incredible how they can light up a black room.

The thought distracts me for a second, but I look back to Amica. She sits on her chair, feet resting on the floor. Her thick black hair is draped on her shoulders in an uneven way. She looks defeated. It's the only word I can use to describe her.

All the slaves are divided into three groups. House, maintenance, and government building. Amica's group is on the far left, so I'm guessing that she's either a government building slave or a house slave. I can only hope for the latter.

A tear begins to build up in my eye. It threatens to burst but doesn't. It stays in its current position.

Amica's face switches between emotions. At first, she looks disappointed, but it's now evolved into anger. A professor walks over to her group, and he begins talking to them. I can't hear what he's saying, but he looks at them condescendingly.

It makes me sick to watch him talk to them that way. These people think they're better because of one test score.

As he finishes his brief talk, I notice that Amica's face has gone pale. Her skin is creamy, tan-like and to see the color drain out from her sends a shiver down my spine.

I swallow nervously, as the professors gather in the center of the stage. Their strides are even, and their chins are up.

Dr. Ashton begins by announcing, "Six Magna Council members."

The next professor continues, "One hundred thirty-two new citizens."

"And finally, one hundred twelve *criminals*," finished a short woman.

"We've improved greatly, but still have a long way to go before our city is free from evil. It is thanks to everybody in this room that we are saving humanity!"

Dr. Ashton clears her throat, and finishes, "Although you may feel insignificant, you are all making history."

It's harrowing that the professors talk in such an excited tone, yet nobody cheers. They all stand quietly, and some scowl towards the new Magna.

Is this how it will be? Am I really a part of the most despised group in history?

My eyes dart from the crowd to Amica. What did she get? I scold myself for thinking of my situation first. I may never know what she gets. If she works in a house, then I'd never get to see her. If she works in the Pura building, I might bump into her as she's cleaning our messes.

As the professors finish the speech, the new Magna Council begins to move. We're escorted out of the balcony, and into an adjacent hallway.

We're led by a few soldiers, dressed in their dark blue uniforms lined with gold. They must be of higher rank due to the logo on their shoulder. It displays the Pura flower, with a triangle around it. Leaves fill the background of the triangle as well.

At the front of that pack is Dr. Ashton. She leads us to the outside of the Pura building, "Since it's so late, you all will go to your normal homes. Tomorrow morning you will be taken back to Purgatio Hall, where you'll be given your living arrangements and money. Then, you'll begin your Magna duties!"

When she is finished talking, we arrive at the sidewalk of the road. Perched along the edge, is a row of limos, one for each Magna Council member.

Dr. Ashton sends us off and we climb into our limos. I choose the one at the back of the line and when I climb in, I'm shocked by the beauty of the interior. The seats are a thick leather, and the windows are dimmed. Crystals line seams where there was probably factory welding.

I begin to tell the driver where to go, but he immediately takes off, following the other cars. I notice candies sitting on a small shelf of the car. As I go to grab one, I remember about Amica. How could I live this life while Amica slaves away?

We arrive at my student housing shortly, and as I leave, the driver rolls down his window and tells me, "I'll be here tomorrow at eight."

His voice has a twangy accent, and it seems to match his gruff face. His short black hair reminds me of my father's.

I thank him, before nodding and walking into my house.

I guess I forgot that they air the scores live, because when I walk in the door, Tabitha is standing in the hallway and rushes in for a hug.

"I'm so proud of you!" she screams. I try to hug back but can't move my arms because she's squeezing me too tightly, "I saw the entire ceremony."

Her expression is giddy, and I find it strange. Why does she accept the system if she's a government slave?

She leads me to the couch, where she forces me to sit. "Tabitha, I really don't want to talk about it."

I get up to leave, but she screams, "Sit back down! I recorded the whole thing, and you're going to watch it!"

My lips tighten, but I sit down anyways because she's not really asking.

She switches the channel from an interview with Dr. Ashton, to the beginning of the ceremony, when we're filing into Purgatio Hall.

The screen is minimized, and a familiar man comes onto the screen. He sits behind a desk, and I recognize him as the city's main reporter. In an authoritative voice, he says, "Today is a great day. An historic event! While the students don't know their scores yet, we do. We have a record size Magna Council this year, consisting of six people. Watch the ceremony now!"

He disappears from the screen as the cameras watch us file into Purgatio Hall. I can already see Dr. Ashton and the others calling out names. I notice myself walking into the hall.

I'm disgusted by the look on my face, I look so nervous. Is this what reporters think when they watch themselves on television?

I watch for a few more minutes and hear Dr. Ashton call out my name. I watch myself trip and fall, and then apologize with a pathetic excuse. Tabitha's face shakes in disappointment.

My focus shifts back to the screen, and I watch the new Magna Council walk to the balcony. The cameras cut from us to the stage, where I instantly see Amica sitting on the far left.

"I'm sorry about Amica, dear," says Tabitha. Her voice is hoarse, and I can tell that she's actually disappointed.

I respond in no way, but instead keep my eyes fixed on the screen—still wishing Amica was sitting next to me now.

I leave the couch, and Tabitha doesn't try to stop me this time.

Chapter 6

MY SLEEP LAST night was often interrupted by nightmares about Amica. I woke up with a rapid heartbeat, and my forehead was sticky with sweat. I searched for my clock but remember that it broke last week. It's still slightly dark outside, so I assume it's early morning.

Downstairs, I can hear Tabitha walking through the kitchen. Since I'm up, there's no point in trying to sleep again. I make my way downstairs.

Tabitha greets me, and gives me a basic muffin, "I work with what they give me." She shrugs as she makes the remark. It makes me wonder if she's a good cook, who works with mostly nothing.

I consume the muffin, and rush back upstairs. My outfit from yesterday was my only nice clothing—I hadn't anticipated getting onto the Magna Council. Since I have no other options, I force myself to wear it again. It feels gross, but there's nothing I can do.

After getting ready, I run downstairs and sneak out the door. As I walk towards the steps, I almost trip over a box on the porch. It's no ordinary cardboard delivery box. It appears to be a safe. The gray exterior is modern, and it's decorated with a golden trim. A foil ribbon is imprinted into the metal and is engraved with my name.

On the front of the box is what seems to be a fingerprint scanner, so I stick my finger in and it comes back positive. The box opens on its own.

Inside the safe is a folded piece of clothing, and I already know that it's a dress. A brand new million-dollar dress. My face forms a smile, and I rush back inside.

I put everything on, and feel rich. The dress is a deep blue skirt, with golden designs spiraling around it. The box also contains some golden bracelets.

A golden Pura flower is embroidered in the right corner of the dress, and golden loops circle around it. As I glance in the mirror, a grin crosses my face at the beauty of the dress.

Satisfied, I make my way out the door, and find the limo sitting outside my house. I walk up slowly, careful not to trip.

A soldier steps out of the limo as he sees me approaching. He opens the door to the car, and says, "Alice Kingston, your driving arrangements will be taking you to Purgatio Hall to get your money and housing."

I nod and lower myself into the limo. I sit in the same seat I did yesterday and try to get comfortable. When the soldier comes back into the car, he shrugs, and I realize I've taken his seat.

I quickly move—trying to make the interaction as least awkward as possible—but the soldier stops me and says, "That won't be necessary Ms. Kingston."

I situate myself back into the seat, and he sits down on the opposite end. He taps his hand against the window towards the driver's seat, and the car begins moving.

We drive at a steady pace and arrive at the school shortly. I climb out of the limo and am immediately greeted by men and women rushing towards me, with cameras flashing.

They try to shout over one another, and I can't make my way through them. Even the soldier has stepped to the side.

This goes on for a minute, before a powerful deep voice comes from behind the reporters yelling, "Let her through!"

They all run out of the way, and the cameras stop flashing. There's now a path between me and the entrance to the building.

The Novus

The only thing in between, is a tall man. He looks around my age, yet he has a wise presence. His thick brown hair curls in luscious waves around his head, and his eyes are a very deep blue. He has broad shoulders and is probably six feet tall. It takes me a second, but I finally recognize him as Oraculi Sceptor. He was on last year's Magna Council and is probably the smartest member they ever had. Since he scored in a certain percentage, he entered the Magna affiliate group where he studied in the field of his choice. That was last month. I vaguely remember him choosing science and medicine. He is the first person to do it.

I walk down the aisle of the crowd, trying to look as confident as possible. I stride all the way up to his side, where another girl my age stands. I'm stunned. She is the girl who was walking around carelessly in the cafeteria. She seemed too confident, but I guess that worked in her favor.

She has a similar build to mine—average height, slim—and similar facial features. The biggest difference is that her hair is blonde, while mine is brown.

Oraculi greets me with his deep voice, "Hello, Alice. I'm sure you know me as Oraculi Sceptor," I nod, and he continues, "On my other side here is Conso Harrington. She is on the Magna Council this year as well."

I nod once again, and he begins walking forward. We follow.

"When do we start?" Asks Conso. I can imagine how Oraculi will respond.

He glares at her before responding, "Soon. Anyways, I will be your mentor for the first few days. Since there were only three people on the Magna last year, and six this year, one mentor will help two new council members."

His words seem clean, precise, and somehow crisp. He wastes no time while speaking and doesn't stutter once.

We continue walking and come upon the long line of people waiting to receive their money and housing. I look at Conso, who displays an irritated look on her face, "Are we going to have to wait in this whole line?"

Oraculi smirks, and chuckles. He turns around, and we both stop walking, "Well, we were going to skip it," Conso's face is relieved, but he continues, "However, Ms. Harrington, I think you need to wait by yourself."

Just like that, we both know what to do. Conso looks even more annoyed, and she joins the end of the line. Oraculi leads me forward. We walk past the long line, and people look at us with disgust. Is this what it will be like? Will people really despise me this much?

I notice that Oraculi doesn't seem bothered by it. I suppose he's used to it by now. We arrive at the door to Purgatio Hall, and squeeze through quickly. They've placed some of the seats back in, as seats for the people who've been waiting in line. Oraculi leads me past the seats, and to a desk near the stage. Behind the desk is a tall woman, with a long nose, and graying hair. I notice a nametag on her jacket but can't quite make out what it says in the dim lighting.

Oraculi greets her, "Good morning, Kareta."

It's not the most enthusiastic greeting, but what surprises me is her name. Kareta is an archaic name from decades ago. Although she has graying hair, she still appears young, "Good morning to you Oraculi." She responds. Her voice is high pitched and comes out as almost a squeak.

He nods, and introduces me, "This is Alice Kingston. A new member of the Magna Council."

"As I suspected," She licks her thumb, and ruffles through some documents before continuing, "You look just like your mother."

The mention of my mother is startling, "You knew my mother?"

"Briefly. I remember when she came to my table to receive her money and housing arrangements."

It seems strange that she would remember such a small interaction, "Do you remember everybody who comes here?" In a split second, I evaluate the thought. It seems unlikely that she would remember everyone, but perhaps she's

45

different in some way. The answer comes into my mind quickly, "Photographic memory, perhaps?"

She chuckles and looks to Oraculi, "She's very perceptive, isn't she?"

He nods. The conversation has ended, and Kareta continues thumbing through the documents for another few minutes.

"Kareta, shall we be here all day? We have a long schedule."

I gulp at the thought of a long schedule. The only thing I've done the past six years is study and go to school, which is a long schedule, but it's also what I'm used to. Kareta ignores Oraculi, and keeps going for another minute before saying, "Mr. Orcauli, please excuse us, her finances are not of your concern." She says it in a mocking tone, and smiles when his face goes red. He walks away. I get a sense that this has happened before. Maybe his mentor was the same and was just as impatient. It seems strange that the wisest person in the city is impatient. Perhaps suppose he's just busy..

She turns back to me, and continues, "Anyways, Ms. Kingston, I had to search your documents twice, because it seems as though you've got a perfect score."

A perfect score? The words hardly sink in, and I'm having trouble displaying emotion, "That can't be possible. Nobody has ever scored perfect."

I can tell that she's disappointed by my reaction. She must have expected me to be extremely excited, but that's the last emotion I'm feeling right now. How could I have possibly scored the highest? It seems improbable. Out of all the people in Pura City for the past six years, how could I have gotten the highest score? Amica's called me a genius, and I typically maintain high scores in all my classes, but that doesn't mean that I'm perfect. Besides, the test isn't only based on academic ability. It's based on how good you are, and if you're likely to engage in criminal activity. So out of all the people, how can I be the best. I'm certainly not the kindest, in fact, I come across as harsh. I remember a cashier telling that to my face one time.

"Alice," she snaps me out of my daze, and continues, "Look, I don't oversee test scores. So, if you have any questions, I recommend you take that up with one of your professors, or someone higher up. But you should be thrilled!"

Kareta is beaming, but I just can't. How am I supposed to be excited? All I've done is secure myself a government job for the remainder of my life.

She continues explaining my test results. The perfect score is five thousand. The average Magna score is four thousand. As she continues talking, she mentions, "You've gotten yourself a role on the government forever! Fame, and riches for the rest of your life."

While she says this, I have to restrain myself from lunging towards her. How can she think I'll want this? *I don't even have a choice.*

Besides, it's not that I don't want money. I'll enjoy my mansion, but it won't be the same. Amica is a slave, and I'll live wonderfully. The cash will certainly be an improvement of my current financial situation, but what's the cost? My life? My friend? That seems to outweigh the value of money, and makes it seem so insignificant.

"There is a series of mansions in the presidential circle for perfect scoring students. They're all currently empty, but they're known as the Houses of Beta."

As she explains, I still think about Amica. I can't possibly live this life while she's a slave. If only I could give her my money.

"Your money situation is around three billion. Two billion is already invested into the city—which is your main source of income."

"What?" She actually repeats what she said, but I cut her off, "I heard what you said, but that can't be possible."

She assures me that it is, and I thank her with every bit of gratitude I contain.

"Of course, dear, but I'm not to thank." She glares at me while saying this.

I glance behind me, and notice Oraculi leading Conso to a table. Her face is red, and I can tell she's angry. As I begin to pull away from Kareta's table, one more question forms inside my mind, "You said I'd have a government position forever. Do you know what it would be?"

She brushes her hair out of her face, before responding, "Well naturally you're in line for Presidency, whenever President Atrox dies."

Now a smirk crosses my face, and I can no longer contain my joy. I'm not happy because of my newfound power. I'm happy because I can use my power to grant Amica immunity to slavery.

Chapter 7

I LEAVE WITH my money card, house key, and confidence. I feel like I've conquered something great. I don't bother to wait for Oraculi or Conso, but instead dash through the hall to the outside.

I'm greeted by reporters once again, but I brush them away while yelling, "No comment."

As I climb into the limo, the driver asks, "To the Pura building?"

I nod my head, and he begins driving. There is a small bit of doubt within my mind. A small voice inside my head that says it's too early to make such demands. It can't be true. Atrox already knows how much power I have, so, why wait a few weeks. I should just do it now, and I'll know the true answer. Surely, he'll trust me. Otherwise, he wouldn't put me in line for Presidency.

We arrive at the Pura building moments later, and I let myself out of the limo before the soldiers could do it for me. Before me, sits a very large building that resembles ancient architecture. The entire building is made from crisp white marble. A giant white staircase leads to a platform with marble pillars extending to an overhang that supports the Presidential balcony. I've never seen it this close before. I've gazed at it from a distance, and on television, but I've never stood at the bottom of the historic staircase. As much as I don't like Pura City, I truly admire its architectural features.

I breathe in, out, and walk to the beautiful staircase. It feels wrong to walk up these stairs. It feels like I don't belong here, and I feel like I'll smear the marble with dirt. As I go higher on the stairs, the building seems to grow. I realize for the first time that the balcony must be sixty feet off the ground. It's amazing that I'll be a part of something so big. I feel so torn. How can I be a part of something I despise, a system that has enslaved my only friend?

As I reach the large platform, a few guards ask for my identification, so I hand them my money card. They verify, and I'm let in quickly. I realize that I've never seen the interior of the building.

Where the Magna Council works. Where the president works. Where anybody important works.

The entrance has an entirely different feel than the exterior. The hallway is decorated in navy blue rugs, with dark hardwood floors below it. The walls are a spotless white and gold marble, with portraits of important figures hanging everywhere. The hall probably stretches twenty feet and is lined with a golden trim.

I feel as though I'm camouflaged into the room with my blue and gold dress. I walk forward to the end of the hall, where a second door stands. They verify my identity once again, and I'm let into the true masterpiece that is the Pura building.

The ceilings are higher, the carpets are gone, and everything is made of white and gold marble. The air within my lunges practically ceases to exist at the beauty of the room. After a minute or so, the air begins to come back to me, and I further examine the hall.

The room stretches seemingly forever, and near the end are dual staircases with a fountain in the middle. Behind the fountain is a large wooden door, and I notice similar ones along the edge of the hallway. I take the first step, and the floor squeaks. The entire building is probably cleaned every single day. The government slaves have a lot of work to do.

I look to the large dual staircases that curve into each other at the top. The platform extends around the edges of the second floor, leaving a very high ceiling. As I search the ceilings, I notice rows of huge golden chandeliers, each one draping down low to fill the space.

I'm trembling with excitement and moving slowly, yet I still reach the staircase soon enough. Surprisingly, no red-carpet lines the staircase, just the bare marble gleaming beneath the lights. I cling to the thin golden railing—afraid that I'll slip on the marble.

Each individual stair is sharp and cleanly cut. The final one smoothly transitions into the second floor. This floor holds larger wooden doors probably three times my height. The only floor of this hall wraps around the edge, leaving a gaping hole in the middle where the chandeliers hang. I can clearly see the first floor, and every new angle offers new beauty.

I walk down the second-floor hall faster than the first, and the hole in the middle closes, leaving a large open area. This must be on top of the entrance hallway. To the left side of the beautiful room, is a huge door labelled *Magna Council*. To the right, is a huge door labelled *Legislative Officers*.

Finally, in the middle of the room is a huge, frosted glass door. In the center—written in gold lettering—is a label saying *Presidential Office*. Along the wall is a row of uniformed soldiers—each standing in unison. Their uniforms are a deep blue, and the seams are lined with gold. Pura's flower holds a spot on each of their caps, and shoulders—along with many badges. They stare into the distance as if I'm not here. One of them stands supporting the Pura flag. It's a simple blue flag, with a golden Pura flower embroidered into it. It sags to the floor due to the lack of wind.

I approach the office, and the guards quickly stop me, "Do you have permission to be here Ma'am?"

It irritates me that they need to validate my identity so many times, "I don't need permission," I bite my lip—hoping I'm not pushing my luck—and hand him my money card.

He squints his eyes while examining the card, "Alice Kingston," he shrugs, "I didn't realize it was you. I'm very sorry." I purse my lips to appear angry with the confrontation, and he quickly backs down. They open the door, and I'm instantly amazed at how each room gets more remarkable.

Glass encased waterfalls spiral through the center of the room, flowing into a large fountain. Bright green plants are placed carefully.

The desk in the center of the room is a dark wood, lined with gold.

Finally, behind the desk is a man. A very ugly man. President Atrox. His nose holds no dimension, and his glasses can barely hold themselves up—not to mention the obnoxiously large size of the glasses. His pale skin is whiter than the marble, and the only thing accompanying his bare face is a wicked smile. A smile that says, *be careful, or I might have to kill you.*

I almost vomit at the sight of him—he's even uglier in real life than on television. I walk towards the desk, until I'm standing directly in front of it. He glares at me, staring me down with eyes more silver than Amica's.

We sit there for what seems like minutes—more uncomfortable for me than for him—before he finally speaks, "Ms. Kingston, It's a delight to meet you, but I don't believe you have an appointment."

I wince at his words. I didn't think how disrespectful this might be to the most important man in the world, "I know that sir, but this was urgent."

"Nothing is urgent enough to waste my time," I gulp when he pauses—unsure if I should speak next. He inspects his fingers, as though he's bored with our conversation already, "But, I'll give you the benefit of the doubt. What do you need?"

"How do you know that I want something? I could just be saying hello." My words are childish compared to his sophisticated tone.

"Alice, I do believe that the smartest person in the world wouldn't be ignorant enough to disturb the President just to say *hello.*"

I swallow nervously. My tongue is dry. Why would I talk back to the President? I finally respond, "Of course, you're right. I'm here to request something."

My palms are sticky, and I begin panting. He asks what I need, and I work up the courage to blurt it out. "I want to grant immunity to the test."

Air slides through my nose, and out of my mouth as I finish the sentence. The reaction that follows is unexpected. He laughs. I thought he might say no, but why is he laughing? His laugh is becoming louder, and I worry that people outside can hear it.

He continues laughing for a minute, before it comes to an end. We're both silent as his eyes reopen from laughing. He stares me down yet again.

After another silent minute, he says, "No."

His face turns cold, and my face grows an angry expression, "She tried her best, she can't possibly be a criminal! Maybe there's a mistake in the grading!"

My voice comes out as a desperate whine, and he replies calmly, "There are no mistakes, and if there were, then the person who made it would be dead."

It's disturbing how he can kill without mercy. I whine once again, pleading for a chance, "There has to be something we can do!"

This quiets him, and he breaks the eye contact. I'm relieved, because I wasn't sure how much longer I could handle it. He stares at the ceiling, the floor, his desk, and finally drags his icy gaze back to mine.

"Alice, I don't think you understand what could happen if we... fudged the system."

I yell back that nobody would know, but he gestures for me to stop talking. He lets out a long sigh and asks who it is. I hesitate to say her name, but decide it's okay to tell, "Her name is Amica Lambert."

"Absolutely not! I know who she is. It's one thing for me to grant immunity to a criminal, but definitely not to the lowest scoring one."

My lips move, but no sound comes out. The lowest? There is no possible way she could have scored that low. That would be below five hundred points! I knew that she wouldn't score very high, but the lowest seems unbelievable, "How could she have scored the lowest?"

"I don't know. All I know, is that I can't have a criminal walking around like a normal person."

My hand slams onto his desk—not realizing how close I am to him, "She is a normal person!" I'm screaming now, but I don't care anymore.

"No, she isn't! I will not have criminals in my city."

I almost respond that he's a criminal, but that would be a death sentence for Amica and I. Instead, I get out of my seat, and begin to walk out. I speed-walk to the door, and a few guards begin opening it when I get an idea. My body automatically turns around, and I walk back to him slowly.

"What if I did something for you?" I speak confidently, enough to make him forget about what we just said.

He looks up at me, "What could you possibly do for me? I have everything I need."

I struggle with the wording, "Except the citizens' agreement with our society," this statement catches him off guard, "You forced us into this system when nobody else wanted it."

"What are you proposing, Ms. Kingston?"

His eyes meet mine yet again, and I hardly know the answer myself. I stutter before stalling while I think, "People have been reluctant of this way of life. Perhaps I could calm them." I'm talking with empty words. The idea is there, but I have no method of execution. I pause—hoping he'll fill in the blanks.

"With speeches?" He responds. I breathe. He's thought of the execution, and it's a good idea. I hadn't thought about it myself, but speeches are better than nothing. I have no other idea, and the clock is ticking, so I nod my head. He seems to be contemplating the idea. I'm not entirely sure how I could pull it off. Atrox himself has done speeches, and he's sent many of his colleagues to do the same. Nothing has worked. However, maybe he's considering it since I got a perfect score.

His skin seems to become paler, and he pushes his glasses up numerous times. Finally, he releases a very long sigh, and declares, "I will let you do the speeches. The system will grant your friend immunity, but only as long as you fulfill your promise."

I nod, trying to subdue my excitement. I didn't underestimate my new power! But it's at a huge cost. It doesn't matter. I'll pay any cost, "Thank you, President Atrox."

"Of course. And I hope you know that the second you fail, your friend will be placed back where she *belongs*." He emphasizes the last word, making sure I understand that she's not the same as the rest of us. But she is the same. Amica is no criminal, no matter what her test score was.

He waves his hand dismissively, indicating for me to leave. The guards open the doors before I get to them, and on the other side I immediately see Oraculi and Conso walking into the Magna room.

How could I have forgotten that I must still be on the Magna Council? And now I just added a speech campaign to the mix. I don't know how I will handle all of this, but I will have to if I want a chance at saving Amica.

I walk out into the marble hall and arrive at the door to the Magna Council room. The door is closed, and two guards stand outside of it.

The soldier on the left opens the door, and I thank her. She replies with a look of disgust on her face. I guess even some of the soldiers don't like the Magna. The thought makes me wonder why they would try so hard to protect us. It's all very confusing. If nobody likes the test except for Atrox, then why do we do it? How can he sustain such a system?

I force myself to stop thinking about this as I walk into the room. I'm immediately underwhelmed. The room is small, and the walls are a dirty gray. There is only one small window on the side leading to the outside. The room feels drafty, and the only thing decorating the wall is a portrait of the first Magna Council member.

He was a horrible person and was despised by everybody in the city. He disappeared four years ago, and there were theories that President Atrox killed him.

In the center of the room is a dark wooden table. Around it is six chairs, five of which are occupied by the new Magna Council.

I take the empty chair—which is closest to the window—and sit down silently. I can feel the cold air drifting into the room. Everybody looks at me. This is the first time I've ever seen my new team closely. I inspect everybody but am interrupted by Oraculi walking back into the room saying, "Hello Alice, you're late."

My chin raises, and I respond, "I was talking with the president." I try not to give too many details.

Conso looks at me—with a distasteful look—and asks, "About what?" I sense a hint of jealousy in her voice.

I struggle to come up with an explanation, but reply, "He was just congratulating me on my score for the test."

Oraculi glares at me doubtfully, but says, "Very well then. Shall we begin?"

I nod and think about what Oraculi has said. He's only one year older than me, yet he seems so wise. Like he's an old man sharing his life experiences in a single sentence. Is this what I'll be like by the end of the year? Will I be so rigid and wise, that I'll act like I'm seventy years old? It's strange to think about my youth disappearing so suddenly.

Two girls walk into the room. I recognize them as Magna Council members from last year. Alium, and Lapis.

Alium begins talking, and she has a totally different presence than Oraculi, "Hello everybody! My name is Alium Lara."

"And my name is Lapis Greiner." Her voice *sounds* like she's rich. And she definitely is. She comes from a long line of businesspeople, each one being successful. She's the first one to be on the Magna instead. The whole thing makes me wonder if strings were pulled, and how accurate the grading really is. But I'm poor, so how would that work?

They continue to introduce themselves, saying pointless facts. It gives me hope for the future. I'd rather be like them than Oraculi.

Finally, Oraculi stops them and says that we must get to work. I can tell that the other new Magna members were bored of the one-sided conversation as well.

Oraculi begins explaining our job, "You all are given the task of making decisions for our society."

"You all have almost as much power as the president."

The more they explain, the worse it gets. Somehow, it seems as though they're trying to make it seem like a horrible job. Sitting in this dark room with the Magna Council for an entire year.

Their introduction to the Magna goes on for hours, and I'm aware that we've missed lunch. I've lost all perception of time—they have no clock because it makes our brains work harder—and I can only hope they'll give us dinner. I'm relieved when Lapis announces, "All right, we'll release you for your dinner. Afterwards, you will report back here where you will spend the rest of the day getting to know each other."

The three old Magna members leave promptly, and we make our way to the cafeteria. They only gave us brief instructions to find our way there.

Down the main hall, down the stairs, through the large hall, door on the left.

We finally find it, and I'm surprised by the small door. We go in. This room is not up to standards with the rest of the building. It's not particularly beautiful. The white tiled floor has many stains from food, and the walls are just concrete.

I make my way to the long line, which is filled with soldiers, and government officials. I'm sure that the higher ranked people get their own room, and the slaves do as well. It makes me wonder why the Magna doesn't dine with them. Perhaps we're not ready yet.

The meal they provide is beautiful. A roasted steak, seared with marks and garnished with vegetables. Sauces decorate the plate, along with green and purple leaves.

We all sit at the same table, but nobody talks. We all keep to ourselves. I'm glad, because I finally have a chance to think about the deal, I made with Atrox. It was all in the heat of the moment, and I'm wondering if I've made the right decision. An entire speech campaign for one person? I probably could've negotiated the price I had to pay. It still seems unlikely that Amica would score the lowest. I knew from the start that she wouldn't be on the Magna—which I thought about myself as well— but being a low scoring slave is horrible. Only now do I realize that since she scored the lowest, she'll work in the Pura building. *Great.* Now I get to live a fancy life, while Amica trails behind me, picking up scraps. All this fuels me, but I'm still not sure about it all. But I stop thinking about it when I realize she would do it for me in a heartbeat.

It seems like an odd coincidence. I scored the highest, and Amica scored the lowest. According to the city, we would be incompatible as friends.

I realize that two of the other Magna members have left the table, and the rest are finishing up their meal. I shove as much as I can down my throat and leave before the last person can. It already feels like I stand out, but not in a good way. The rest of the Magna Council must see me as an outsider, considering my perfect test score.

I remove the thought from my mind and walk to the Magna room quickly. I'm glad that I had the meal. Not only did I get a filling steak, but it gave me a chance to clear my mind and think about all that's happened. I think back to yesterday morning. If only I could go back and warn myself about all of this. If only I could have been more prepared.

However, that wouldn't have helped me. Amica would still be a slave, and I wouldn't be able to do anything about it. I have to think like Amica and shove myself aside. This is for her, and I'll get what I want.

I arrive at the Magna room and sit down in the same seat as before. Everybody is silent, and the last person walks in shortly after me. Nobody talks for a few minutes, although I can tell they want to. Nobody knows where to start.

"My name is Nita." The voice is soothing and comes from a tall athletic looking girl. Her skin is very tan—almost orange. I had a cousin named Nita. It is an ancient name and is hardly ever in use anymore. My cousin Nita died in the war at the age of nineteen.

I examine Nita more and try to deduce her personality. Her voice is upbeat, and I can already tell that she's kind.

One by one we all introduce ourselves. Zane— a slim, but very tall boy—and Zed—a tall, slightly chubby boy, with dark hair like mine.

The two other girls are Conso and Avetay— who appears to be half my height. So far, I like Nita and Avetay the most. Conso looks at me with jealousy, and Zane isn't particularly interested in anybody. He seems to have a rebellious nature. Zed and Conso were neighbors before the war, and they're practically brother and sister.

After all of this, a guard comes in and finally allows us to leave. On the drive to my new house, I think about my mother. What would she think of me right now? I'm living a rich lifestyle, and I'm not allowed to share it.

I truly hope that I haven't disappointed her. If she was here, I can't help but feel that she would be. I'd never be able to live with myself if I did.

By the time I finish reminiscing, the driver pulls into the Presidential circle. I've seen it on television, but it's even more beautiful. Five mansions sit around a huge circle accompanied by a glistening fountain in the middle. Although it's night, they've lit the houses with bright lights. It's breathtaking, and I wonder how it's put together.

On the far side of the fountain—in the middle—is the Presidential house. The architectural style of it is similar to the Pura building. A large marble structure, with a huge staircase. Pillars extend from the platform at the top of the stairs, and the doors are huge.

However, I'm not here for the president's mansion. I glance to the left, where my house sits on a huge lot. One of four Beta houses. It's almost as big as the president's mansion, but I display no reaction. I can't, for Amica's sake.

A soldier opens the limo door and offers his hand to help me out. I note that he's a military specialist. The right shoulder of his uniform is decorated with a golden pauldron, with a specialist seal on it. The seal is a triangle with a golden Pura flower inside.

As I climb out of the limo, the colors brighten from the dim windows, and my house seems bigger. A wide staircase leads to a beautiful platform with pillars stretching to the ceiling. These pillars aren't smooth like the others, but instead are intricately carved. While I ascend the staircase, my eyes dart from place to place, taking in the scenery. The landscaping is completely symmetrical on both sides of the staircase, each decorated with green bushes, bright flowers, and crystal-clear fountains.

I mount the platform and turn around to take in the beauty one more time. I watch the limo driving to a garage down the street. The entire sight is beautiful. It's a shame that the other Beta houses are wasted. For now.

If only Amica were here to see this. I inhale slowly, and exhale as I turn and make my way to the frosted glass doors.

Two soldiers open the large doors, and I'm impressed instantly. I thought that the outside was nice, but nothing could have prepared me for the interior.

I immediately walk in and take off my shoes, hang up my coat, and set down my bag. My gaze can't stay focused because the entire room is decorated with breathtaking decorations. White marble floors, stained wooden tables, golden pillars, and glass encased waterfalls. I can hear the subtle dribble of water folding into itself, only to be circulated back to the top to go again.

Dual staircases with golden railings lead to a balcony that overlooks the masterpiece. I walk forward and find myself in what appears to be the living room. A huge window descends from the ceiling to floor. It's interesting how they create fake windows. You couldn't see this from the outside.

I settle onto a beautiful blue and gold couch and find a remote sitting on a coffee table below me. I'm confused, there appears to be no television screen. I grip the remote in my hand and press the power button—hoping for a reaction.

Suddenly, the huge window dims to black, and the screen turns to a huge selection of movies and television shows. I scroll through but decide to explore more of the house before settling down for the night. I hoist my body from the comforts of the couch and continue on through the house.

The next room is the kitchen. It's breathtaking, and I wish I'd had more time to examine it when I notice somebody sitting on a stool at the island. Their back is turned towards me.

The body sits quietly, and I examine them. It's obviously a girl, their hair is tucked into a sweatshirt. It's a shiny black. Her hand drops to the base of the stool, and I notice a bracelet. Just as I place their identity, they greet me, "I was wondering when you would get home."

Amica.

"Amica, what are you doing here?" Of course, I know the answer, but she can't know that I'm protecting her. Yet.

She turns around and says, "They messed up my score. I scored average." Her eyes have kept the gray color from the ceremony, and her voice doesn't match her tone. I dread what she'll say next.

"Well, that's great!" I respond—trying to end the conversation.

She responds hastily, "Yeah! The flawless system messed up a simple task."

At the end, her voice drops into a low register, and I break, "Amica, I'm sorry, but I couldn't let you be a slave while I rule the city."

I sigh due to her quick discovery, and she snaps, "Well, you should have talked to me about it first! People think that you gave me immunity!" Her voice has become angry, and raised to a shout, "How am I supposed to live it up while the rest of them serve me! Why would you only save me?"

"I could hardly get you immunity. I have to do an entire speech campaign. I could barely save you, and you expect me to save thousands?" My voice remains calm—I vaguely remember reading once that staying calm in an argument helps you win. Although I'm still mad. She has no right to make me feel this way. I saved her from life as a slave!

"I would have rather you talked to me about it! You think I can just flip a switch after what they've done?"

"Amica, you were only there one day, how much has happened?"

"One boy tried to run, so they're putting him in Pura's dungeon management."

I'm about to yell back, but my voice has disappeared. No argument I make could go against that. How can they treat people like this?

We sit in silence after her words, and she finally asks about my deal with Atrox, "I have to make speeches to convince people that our lives are perfect."

"Do you think it's possible? Atrox himself has tried, and it never worked."

"I know that" I pause before continuing, "But he'd never agree unless he thought I could do it."

"Alice, you should have done less. Why would you do this just for me?"

The small string of words takes me back eleven years. She had just come to our refugee camp from Canada after her father was shot down in a bomber plane.

This refugee camp was in a state formerly known as Kansas—which is now Pura City— which was right in the center of the United States. Over the next few years, we became friends. My father had died at this point, and my mother was doing refugee volunteer work.

The soldiers held off bombers until we finally won the war. Kansas turned into Pura City, and Atrox remained the president. The Purification occurred when we were twelve.

I collect my thoughts and create the sincerest string of words I can manage, "Amica, nothing I do is ever *just* for you. You're my friend, and if I

let you be a slave, I could never live with myself.
It's not for you. It's for us."

Chapter 8

AMICA LEAVES, AND I find ice cream inside the freezer. My mother told me that it's a great way to clear your head. As I eat, I think about the speech campaign. How can I possibly pull this off?

If President Atrox can't do it, how can I? How could anybody create a speech that satisfies everybody's needs? To make matters worse, it's coming from me. Of course, people would think I liked the test. It worked in my favor.

What's really wrong with the system, anyway? I know it's wrong to make people slaves, but the crime rate is almost zero percent. Besides, anybody who commits a crime automatically becomes a slave. Either way, crime is almost unheard of nowadays.

The Novus

The more I think about it, my face freezes. I drop the spoon that was on track for my mouth. How can I think like this? I can't possibly think that this test is okay. While it takes away crime, it enslaves innocent people! How could I forget my philosophy? *Innocent until proven guilty.*

I feel my face go red, but it eases as tears roll down my cheeks. The tears continue flowing, leaving stains on my face.

The phase comes when the crying stops, and I begin to shake. It's happened to me before, and we were never sure why. My entire body shakes, and I have no control. Soon, I fall onto the floor. It's like a balloon inside me, threatening to explode.

However, I didn't expect the balloon to be real. I'm vomiting on the ground before I can stop myself. I rush around the mansion, searching for a bathroom.

I find one in a nearby hallway. Over the next hour, I'm hunched over the toilet. At least the bathroom is beautiful. I force myself to think about the beauty of the house, rather than what I'll throw up next.

When I stop throwing up, I exit the bathroom. A nearby slave directs me towards my bedroom. A few soldiers open the door for me, and I instantly love the room.

The room is still themed blue and gold, and anything that isn't those colors is white marble.

The bed has a navy-blue comforter, and a golden blanket at the end. The posts on the bed are marble and lead up to blue curtains draping over the bed.

Each wall is decorated with decadent tapestries, each one containing a piece of history. I like to think it's amazing how people can weave history.

One tapestry catches my eye, so I examine it. I begin looking at the whole thing, but so much is going on that it's too difficult to decipher.

In the middle is an adult man—probably forty years old—who is rather slim and has pale skin. He wears an outfit that is prewar style. A black suit, with a red tie. His shoes are black, sleek, and pointy.

The troubling part of the tapestry is what happens around him. Only now do I realize. Many missiles, swords, and guns all point towards the man. I finally realize who that man is. Prince Atrox. President Atrox's brother.

There are a lot of things I don't like about him, but first is his name. He wasn't even a prince. He was a king, yet his name was Prince.

Prince was the leader of the other half of the world. He dominated the eastern hemisphere, but our soldiers were stronger. We held them off, and President Atrox overpowered his brother.

After the war—during the Purification— President Atrox killed his brother. The biggest execution in history. All because of a war that killed billions of people.

It's also the only reason anybody respects our president. Prince was despised.

I examine the tapestry for a few more moments, before I turn away and go to bed. When I reach the bed, I'm comforted by the way the mattress hugs me. It's certainly an improvement from the student mattress.

I order the slaves out of the room, and request for them to turn out the lights.

When they finally leave, I try to fall asleep.

The next morning, I awaken to a slave who tells me I'm five minutes late. I thank them, and groan when they leave. It takes me ten minutes to get ready, and I dress myself in a black dress.

I'm forced to skip breakfast and leave at once—knowing I'm late. When I reach the bottom of the staircase, I see the limo parked in front of the house. I notice that it's a different limo—the design is slick and reflects the modern style of cars more clearly.

I climb in, and notice that the driver is different as well. He is a small man, with short arms. I wonder if his legs are short as well, and if that would affect his ability to reach the gas pedal. I can't see his face, but the back of his head is covered in blonde hair, that fades to a hole in the middle. I'd estimate his age above fifty.

He grunts as he begins to drive, and we make our way to the Pura building.

When I exit the car, I can't help but notice protesters on the side of the road next to the building. Men, women, and even some teenagers all stand together holding signs. They scream, but the soldiers stand unphased.

I wonder how the teenagers are here but remember that students are off for a few days after the test. Except for the Magna Council, and slaves. I enjoyed those times when I was younger. I'll never get to do it again.

I try my best to ignore them as their screams rise when they see me. The soldiers let me into the building, and I make my way down the hall quickly trying to not stop and observe the beauty of the hall.

When I reach the second floor, I quicken my pace, and arrive at the Magna Council's door.

I take a deep breath as the guards open the door. When I walk in, I get the same underwhelmed feeling as last time. The drafty feeling in the room reminds me that not everybody lives with amazing conditions. Although it still takes me by surprise that we aren't given the finest living conditions. Not that it matters.

When I take my seat, I glance around the room. Everybody has arrived except for Zed. It's three minutes past start time, and it surprises me that he would be this late.

The Novus

We all sit in silence, nobody talking to each other. Conso attempts to open the folder in front of us, but Nita stops her and says we should wait. She nods, but I can tell that she's anxious to begin.

The three mentors walk in, and only now do I realize they were late as well, "Sorry that we're late, the protesting outside is becoming violent, and it's difficult to get through when you're one of the most despised people in the city." Says Oraculi, with a sigh.

We all nod. I glance at Nita, and notice a nervous look on her face before she asks, "You don't think Zed got caught up in the protesting, do you?"

Nobody answers her, but instead the worrying expression on our faces grow.

Ten more minutes pass by—I think—and Zed still hasn't shown up. Lapis suggests a search team, right as Zed walks through the door.

His hair is rugged, and I notice several scratches on his face. I observe that his shoes are slightly squished down, and his clothing is ripped in various spots. All of this is distracting me from the large red stain on his shirt.

"What happened to you?" Conso asks, teasingly. I'm not sure how she could find this funny.

Zed locks eyes with her, and I watch Conso shrink before he responds, "You know what happened to me? My driver didn't show up this morning, so I had to walk here. I was greeted by protesters outside the building. One of them sliced my arm open!" He roars, as he reveals a nasty wound.

The cut is still spraying blood, and it goes pretty deep. The three mentors gasp in horror at the sight, but for some reason, the Magna Council remains silent. I get a strange feeling that he can't display enough anger on his face. He sits down, and that's the end of the conversation.

Nita finally allows us to open the folders on the table. Inside of each of the folders are small digital tablets. We power them on and read it silently in our heads. It reads:

Assignment from President Maxwell Atrox II:

Dear Magna Council, your very first assignment is to redirect the protesters from the government building. I'm sure you all saw Zed. I've already passed a new law that requires protesters to only participate in the activity on approved grounds. You are to create ideas for spaces to move them, and then put it into action.

I pause, and let the words sink in. How did he already know about Zed? How did it get into the folders that have been sitting in front of us this whole time? Then, it hits me. Atrox could have stopped Zed's limo, and then he'd have no other choice but to walk through the protesters. All of that just to make a point. I wonder if the others have figured that out. I stop thinking about this, because I know I must start making decisions.

Everybody is looking around, thinking about the assignment, so I try to focus and do the same.

Where could we move them? Before I can think anymore, Zed says, "We should just remove their right to protest. Pass a law."

"No," Zane snaps, firmly, "It would only make them angrier. Besides, they should have a voice, just like us."

"Why? They sliced me open!"

"It's not all about you! These people feel as though they need to be heard."

Oraculi raises his hand—indicating for them to stop arguing—and says, "Alright. While this discussion is good for making decisions, it's your first mistake. To be efficient, you must work cooperatively."

They both nod, and quieten. I glance towards Avetay, who has been on a computer this whole time. I ask what she's doing.

"I'm searching for an empty lot," she begins, "I've expanded the search radius to one mile, and there are two options."

She pushes her computer to the center of the table and presses the screen to the tabletop. Her fingers graze a few buttons, and a hologram appears. I've never seen a hologram before.

Inside of the hologram, is a city map, "Here is the Pura building," She says, pointing to it on the map, "We need to keep them close enough that they feel heard, but far enough that they don't cause damage."

The three mentors nod in agreement.

Avetay zooms in on the hologram to a small plot of land, "This is the first option. The owner currently has plans to turn it into a wrestling complex."

We all examine it, and Lapis says, "It's an odd shape. It should be more of—"

Oraculi cuts her off, "Lapis, this is their decision."

She apologizes and claims it's force of habit.

"Anyways, that was my thinking as well. So, this one would probably be better," She zooms out, and then moves into another empty area, "They were planning to build military barracks here. It's huge, and a square. It's government owned, so we could easily take it."

"But what about the soldiers? Where would they stay?" Asks Zane.

I chime in quickly, "The plans could be postponed, and we could make a waiting list. Or they could move to a different area. It would take years to build, so they aren't expecting any soldiers yet."

Everybody nods. Oraculi observes me with a wise look.

Alium congratulates Avetay and I on the idea, and asks how we'll do it, "We'll use soldiers to escort them to the lot. We can make a traffic detour as well." Responds Zane.

We all nod once again and get to work. Making the road detour plan, organizing a group of soldiers to execute the task, and shutting down three streets.

Once we've finished the idea phase, we move on to the action phase—as Oraculi calls it. We send a written plan to President Atrox, and he responds with a kind note saying that it sounds good.

We contact a military commander and tell him to send a group of soldiers. Finally, we organize the event so that a city representative can make the announcement over the city's speakers.

Two hours later, the representative echoes through the speakers, "To all the protesters outside the Pura building, you will be redirected to another lot due to the violence you've displayed. Effective immediately."

There's a muffled noise as she sets down the microphone, and a loud beep occurs. Oraculi turns on a television and sets it to the live viewing of the escort.

We watch as soldiers lead the front people forward and push the stragglers in the back. They move steadily and show no signs of resistance. I hear Avetay sigh in relief.

The escort lasts for about an hour, and they finally arrive at the empty lot. It's a beautiful lot with bright green grass, and a park surrounding it.

Oraculi turns off the television with a click, and it returns to the black screen. The room has an eerie silence to it, but I break it by blurting out, "President Atrox has insisted I do a speech campaign. I have to take off tomorrow so I can prepare." The words just come out, and I'm not even sure why I told them. Perhaps to inform them of my absence, or to gain reassurance.

Everybody's faces display shock while the words sink in, as I expected. Conso responds in a jealous tone, "Why is he letting you do it? What's it even about?"

They all bombard me with similar questions, and I cut them off by responding, "The speeches are to convince people that our city is perfect. To stop the protesting and convince them that our lives are great."

"Hardly," mutters Zane. I'm the only one that hears it.

"Sounds good to me." Says Zed. Conso shoots him a dirty look.

"Why aren't you all doing it?" Asks Alium.

I shrug, as if I don't know the answer. I do, but the story I gave them wouldn't match up with the truth. I glance at Conso, whose face is either red with anger, or blushing with embarrassment.

The Novus

I try to read the room. Nita and Avetay sit quietly in their seats, seemingly content with their position. Zane is now quiet as well and looks as though he's forcing back tears. I wasn't expecting this much of a reaction from them.

I clench my jaw and squeeze my hands tightly. They must sense the tension I'm giving off, because the conversation is now over.

We all sit awkwardly, waiting for somebody else to speak first. Nobody does, so eventually Zane gets up and walks out of the room.

Chapter 9

WE ALL FOLLOW with similar actions. I leave second to last, with Oraculi behind me. When I walk out of the room, I don't see any of the other Magna Council members ahead of me.

I walk in the hallway, and down the stairs. When I exit the building, I'm glad to see that my limo is already there, and the others have left. I realize that Oraculi won't have a limo anymore. Nobody really thinks about what happens after the Magna Council. What do they do? They have tons of money, so they probably retire. They no longer have limo escorts everywhere. Every past Magna member is no longer famous and can go on living the lives they lived before. They're kicked out of their mansions and put into normal citizen housing.

The thought scares me, but I don't know why. Why should I care about them? I am one of them now, and it's not like I'll ever leave the government. I scored the highest, so I must pay the price. The price is my life.

My life isn't really mine anymore. It belongs to the city, and how it plays out is also the city's decision. I'm a public figure whether I like it or not.

After collecting my thoughts, I look over my shoulder, where I see Oraculi walking down the stairs. He looks awfully stressed. The sunlight beams down on him, and you can see his hair all out of place. He fidgets his hands nervously, and his steps are short. He would probably look a lot better if he wasn't carrying the weight of the city on his shoulders.

A thought crosses my mind, and before I can think about it anymore, I call out, "Oraculi!" I've caught his attention, and he begins to make his way over, "Do you need a limo ride?"

I'm not sure why I want to help, but it feels like I should.

He chuckles before responding, "That's very kind of you, but my Magna Council days are over. I'm afraid you have a tight schedule, and you don't need to put me on it."

My face goes red with embarrassment. I've defied my own logic. *Think before you act.* But somehow, I couldn't stop myself.

He begins walking away. A few steps in, he turns around and locks his eyes on mine, "You can call me Eli. It's what most people call me."

Eli. The name is nice. The red on my face begins to drain, and it feels like I've won something. But what?

For just a split second, I saw Oraculi—Eli, for who he really is. He's only one year older than me, and this is the first time I've seen him act like it.

He moves away from me and walks to a nearby parking lot. My breath quickens, and I climb into the limo. I realize that the original driver has returned. He's considerably taller than the blonde one, and his hair is a very dark brown. I'd place his age at around fifty.

"Could you wait a few minutes while I find a private assistant?"

He nods, "I know one. The best one." His voice is very deep, and he sounds powerful.

The limo begins to move, and I hope that he's taking me to a good private assistant. I would have preferred though he told me the place so I could look it up.

We drive for thirty minutes, and a sensation of fear grows within me as the scenery changes. He takes the limo to the outskirts of Pura. I know it's wrong to judge an entire population, but it's the outskirts. The outskirts of Pura where the real criminals are. They are never caught, but the government has an unspoken agreement to leave them alone. Lots of them are immigrants, and the rest are simply homeless.

I've never seen the outskirts before, but it has an entirely different feel than the rest of the city. A hazy yellow hue fills the skies, and everything seems dirty. The houses are made of a dark wood, and smoke rises from various parts of the town. I can see the city wall from here.

On the right side of the limo is a string of houses, and on the left is a few shops. The front signs look beaten, and most of them are covered in graffiti.

He slows the speed of the limo, and glances around nervously—as if he's expecting an attack.

Instead, three children run out in front of the car, and he immediately stops driving. They stop in the center of the road, and stare directly at us. I look towards the driver—who appears to be agitated.

The kid on the left is probably ten years old. He wears rags, and his hair looks like a bird's nest. The child in the middle is an older boy, probably fourteen years old. He has greasy brown hair, and large brown eyes.

The child on the right is what strikes fear into my soul. She is a little girl, probably six years old.

She wears a rag dress, that curls around her emaciated body.

My eyes widen, and my mouth opens as I yell, "Don't move the car!"

I open the door and climb out quickly. The driver yells behind me, but I don't stop. I run towards the children—specifically the little girl. Inside my pocket is a bulging wallet, and I give her as much money as I can. I'm not sure how much I give her, but it should be more than enough to fill the void that should be her stomach.

A smile crosses my face, and I say, "Go buy some food. Please." I'm pleading, and begging, as though the tone of my voice could decide if she lives or dies.

The girl looks up to me and locks her eyes on mine. She opens her mouth—where a gap from lost teeth is—and says, "Do you have any more?"

I begin to get out my wallet again, but I fall to the ground immediately. A powerful force shoves me, and I realize it was the older boy. He pins me down, while the younger boy grabs my wallet. I feel a weak kick on my shin from the little girl, and they all run off laughing.

It all happens too fast for me to process. Why would they do that? I probably gave that little girl enough to buy a house!

I hoist myself from the ground and begin chasing them down. They're probably fifty feet away, and I know that I'll never make it. Just as I'm about to stop, something else stops me. The driver. He lifts me a few inches off the ground and turns me around. At first, I thought he was attacking me, until he whispers into my ear, "Get in the car, and do what I say."

He drops me to the ground, and I immediately run to the car. I climb into the back as he climbs into the front. The second he sits, he begins driving while explaining, "You should have just sat down. It's very dangerous out here."

"What is this place?"

He glares back towards me and stops the car. Then, he turns around so that he's facing me, "You really want to know?" I nod my head, "This is Malus town. All they do is fight for scraps."

"How do they live poorly? Doesn't the government distribute the money equally?"

His fist smashes into the center of the steering wheel before responding, "Do they still tell you that? How do you think there are homeless people? They don't distribute anything evenly."

He says nothing more, and begins driving again, "How do you know about this place," I clear my throat before rephrasing, "I mean, how do you know how to... navigate it."

He snickers, "Came here after the war."

A crunching sound occurs, and I realize that we've pulled into a gravel driveway. He orders me out of the car and doesn't follow.

Before I continue walking, I turn around and ask, "What's your name?"

He glares towards me, and replies, "Ordell."

I wish he'd give me a last name, but I decide to not push any further.

I continue my walk and go slowly up an unbeaten path. Before me is a small house, made of old rotting wood. Some sections fade into a mossy green, while others fade into empty holes where windows should be.

I walk up a few creaky stairs and come upon the front door. This door is probably the brightest feature of the property. It is a dull red, and I wonder if it symbolizes anti-Pura colors. Red and white unofficially symbolize protesting Pura City. I'm sure the wood used to be white before it rotted.

Next to the door is a sign that says, *Auxillio's Assistant Services.* I knock on the door, curious, and hear some shuffling feet inside. I hear whispers between people, one muttering, "Doesn't anybody know what a doorbell is?"

I shrug, and as I do, the door opens. I expected a small old lady, dressed in rags, but instead am greeted by a vibrant middle-aged woman dressed in a red and gold pantsuit. Her outfit is brighter than her front door.

The woman in front of me is slim and has a long nose. Her eyes are a bright blue, and her lips are decorated with a bright red lipstick.

A huge smile crosses her face—displaying all of her teeth—before greeting me, "Welcome! Come in!"

She maintains eye contact, and I can't help but feel uncomfortable. When I walk in, I avert my eyes, and lead them to two identical twins dressed in matching dresses. Their hair is brown like mine; however, their eyes are different colors. Blue, and almost orange.

"I'm Auxillio. This is Mory and Nory," she gestures to the two women, "They're my assistants. How wonderful is that? You're going to have an assistant with assistants!" She belts out a laugh that reminds me of opera music.

I walk deeper into the room and observe the living conditions. Even my student housing was nicer than this. I can't help but ask questions, "Why doesn't the government give you guys housing out here?"

Auxillio sighs, as if she's heard it before. She stares at me while saying, "All of us here in Malus town didn't make it into *real* Pura City. We're forced out here, where the government gives us nothing."

"That's terrible." I say.

"It's not so bad. There's hardly any government control around here. Besides, we built up this business, and now we live fine." Explains one of the twins.

I nod my head and realize that it doesn't sound bad at all. A question pops into my mind, and I know it's disrespectful, but I ask anyways, "Do they have you take the test out here?"

All three of them stare at me simultaneously before Auxillio replies, "Some of us. Others squeak by. The government doesn't know some of us exist. Our parents hid us before they could ruin our lives."

I nod my head, and one of the twins asks, "So, what kind of assisting do you need?"

"I'm on special orders from President Atrox to do a speech campaign. In order to calm the protests." I explain.

They all nod, except for Auxillio who yells, "Get out!"

Surprised, I ask why.

"Why? I don't want any government business here! Malus town has survived for six years without..." She trails off and I can see her perk up again, "You're here to shut down Malus town, aren't you?"

"She's probably from the Magna Council. She said she's on orders from Atrox." Says one of her assistants.

I struggle to come up with a response, even though their idea of what I'm doing here isn't true.

Auxillio begins walking towards me slowly, and I notice the twins closing in as well, "We don't want any government or Magna Council business here. I don't care about your speech campaign. Why else would you be here? Why would a rich girl like you come to Malus town for my assistance?" Asks Auxillio.

I retreat, knowing they're going to attack. But I know it's not criminal behavior, it's more like self-defense. Other people fear the government too. It makes me forgive them for their hostile behavior, but what if they attack me?

They're getting closer, and I wonder what they'll do. Whatever it is, it will harm me. My mind races as I try to think of a way to get out. One of the twins is blocking the door, and they're probably faster than me anyways.

One thought comes to my mind, but I can only hope it will work, "Ordell sent me."

And suddenly the tension within the room ceases to exist, and they all back off. I take a breath and remind myself that they're good people. Good people, who were put in a bad place. Growing up on the streets certainly gives you trust issues.

I don't know why I thought that Ordell's name would help me, but something tells me that there's a deeper connection between them.

"Ordell sent you," repeats Auxillio, "How do you know Ordell?"

"I could ask you the same."

"I asked you first."

I hesitate to respond, because somehow, it feels like secret information, "He's my limo driver."

Auxillio walks to an old table with a broken leg, and sits down with a sigh, "Ordell is a lot of things, but I never expected him to be a driver."

"You know him?"

I can tell that Auxillio doesn't want to share the information, but she does anyways, "Ordell came here after the war. I don't know everything, but that man certainly keeps a lot of secrets."

It seems disappointing to hear that. I'm not sure why, but it felt like I could trust him. I realize that I'm in search of people I can trust.

"Well, what do you know?" I feel the need to find out.

"He has a way of hiding and getting away with things." She glances to the twins, and they all seem to be hiding something, "What's your name?" she asks—obviously trying to switch the topic.

"Alice Kingston." Auxillio gulps and winces in one motion.

Before I can ask about the strange reaction, one of the twins—Nory, I think—says, "Back to what we were talking about. You need assistance with a speech campaign?"

"To calm the riots." I respond. So, I tell them everything. The real story. I tell them how it's to save Amica, and how I lied to the rest of the Magna

94

Council. I even tell them about Atrox's expectations.

Auxillio eases even more when she realizes I'm doing it for a friend, "Well, that's very kind of you. Very *un-Magna* behavior."

I nod, because it's true. I really don't want to be on the Magna Council.

Over the next few hours, we discuss the matter. We talk about how we can accomplish the speeches, and how we could settle the riots.

"I'm on annual leave tomorrow so I could plan. I was hoping that you could come to my house so we could talk about it."

"Of course." Says Auxillio.

As I get ready to leave, before Mory says, "Wait, there's one more thing. We have to discuss our price."

They all seem interested in the topic, until Nory responds, "Don't be ridiculous, Mory. She's on the Magna Council. She could give us millions."

I shrug, give a small wave, and walk out the door.

I'm glad to see Ordell sitting in his seat, waiting intently for my arrival. I climb into the back, and he asks, "How'd it go?"

"Fine. They're coming to my house tomorrow to help me plan."

He nods and begins to drive. About halfway to my house, he asks, "So what exactly do you need planned?"

It feels wrong to give Ordell information after Auxillio's description of his ability to keep secrets. Yet he asks a direct question. I can deflect it back onto him after my answer, "I'm doing a speech campaign to calm the riots," He nods, and I decide to press further, "How do you know Auxillio?"

"I told you—kind of. I came here after the war."

"But what did you—"

He cuts me off, "I wasn't considered *high value* to the government anymore. They put me into Malus town. That's where I met Auxillio. She found out about my skill set and requested my help with a project she was working on."

I'm about to ask for more, but sense that I should stop. There's a deeper relationship going on here, but it doesn't feel like my space to pry. Yet it does at the same time. Why else would he tell me this? Perhaps I'm connected to the story somehow.

I realize that he's pulled up to my house, so I climb out. I walk forward without looking back, but I can hear the limo driving away.

It seems weird that just a few days ago, I lived in student housing. I walk up the steps that seem as though I've had them my entire life.

I'm let in the doors by the guards, and I walk straight to my bedroom. I'm exhausted. At this point, it is past midnight, and I need to rest so I can make the speech tomorrow.

The Novus

I crash into my bed and fall asleep without a second thought.

Chapter 10

I WAKE UP to a slave who informs me, "Somebody named Auxillio is waiting downstairs."

Confusion crosses my face before the words sink in. I nod and get ready. I'm glad to be home today—I can finally wear normal clothes.

I run downstairs quickly and find Auxillio and her assistants sitting on the living room sofa, "Ah! There you are Alice."

Today, she wears a bright pink pantsuit, and she wears makeup that matches the pink. I wonder if she switches colors every day. It also makes her stand out. Nobody else dressed in bright colors like her.

I return her greeting, and then lead them to a study in the mansion. I take a seat at the desk, while

The Novus

Auxillio sits across from me in a chair. Mory and Nory sit a few feet away on a small couch.

"So, we need to get right to work. We only have today to prepare your speech, and I don't want it to be a late night. You must be rested for tomorrow."

We begin immediately, and she gets right to work brainstorming ideas. We don't mention it, but we both know that it will be difficult to convince people that the city is perfect. It's far from perfect, and neither of us are loyal to the system.

She pulls up a program on her computer that can help organize and write speeches. She claims she uses it all the time for big clients and celebrities. I find it hard to believe considering that she lives in Malus town though. Not that celebrities make much more than normal citizens anyways.

In Pura City, a child's time is taken by constant schooling. Adults usually have a job—if they scored average—but don't make much extra cash. Celebrities are just average scoring people whose names happen to be known.

I force myself to stop thinking about celebrities and focus on Auxillio. She's typing in her speech program and talking about the speech. I don't think I've missed too much, so I continue following along.

"What I've found is that in the beginning, you really have to captivate their attention with a brilliant point!" she explains. Has she really been working on the first line for ten minutes? This will take longer than I thought.

She continues talking about how the hook is important, and after thirty minutes, she claims that she finally came up with a good one.

She reads it aloud. When she's finished, she looks at me with a huge smile, and I can see the hope in her eyes. I'm not a fan of Pura City, so I don't like it. However, if I killed the flicker of hope inside Auxillio, then what hope would there be for the rest of us?

"I like it!" I assure her, trying to not sound pathetic.

She squeals in excitement, and releases an unexpected scream, "This is going to be easier than I thought!"

It's going to be a long day.

Over the next few hours, we continue creating and refining the speech. We work until ten at night, and when we're finished, I've almost brainwashed myself into thinking Pura City is perfect.

I nearly go through the crying and vomiting again but hold it back for Auxillio's sake.

She informs me that tomorrow we are on a tight schedule. It will be practicing all day, and then presenting the speech. My stomach churns at the thought of speaking in front of the entire city. It goes against my entire identity. I tend to close off all my ends and stay quiet. This speech may be a shock to the few people who know me.

I stop thinking about this, and try to get Auxillio out, "Alright, well I guess I should get some sleep."

She hesitates—as if she can sense what I'm doing—and says, "Of course."

She gives me a brief hug, and then walks out the door.

The guards close the doors behind her, and I sigh in relief. I quickly make haste for my bedroom and go right to bed.

My alarm goes off at five in the morning.

It's tough to get up, but I do anyways. I shower, and then dress myself in rags. Auxillio tells me that she found a nice dress from a designer in Malus Town.

I run downstairs—aware of the fact that I'm on a tight schedule—and try to finish breakfast before six A.M.

Auxillio barges in the front door, "Come on now Alice, it's time to go."

She practically drags me out the door.

We walk down the large staircase, and into a limo. I look to the driver, and notice that he is the blonde one again. He begins to drive—going noticeably faster than Ordell.

Auxillio sits on the seat opposing mine. She wastes no time, and instantly says, "We're on a tight schedule."

I nod, as if I didn't know this already. It feels like Auxillio is always seeking my approval. I wish she didn't.

"We will arrive at the government building in around five minutes. Once there, we will practice presenting the speech up until eleven."

"Is that when we start the speech?"

"No, don't cut me off," she says harshly. I can see the stress in her eyes as she says, "Sorry, I don't mean to come across as rude."

"It's alright."

"Anyways, at eleven, we will eat a quick lunch. We will then go back to the drill room, and practice for about two more hours." She pauses slightly, before adding, "And then we will start the speech."

I nod, and a few seconds later, we pull up to the Pura building. Before I get out, I breathe in, and try to comprehend that this is the last time I'll be looking at it without being a part of it.

I exhale as I climb out of the limo. Reporters are running at me before I can take two steps. I'm confused about how I couldn't see them before.

"Ms. Kingston, how do you plan to calm the riots with a speech?"

Many reporters ask questions like this, but I ignore them and push through while saying, "No comment."

I try to sound nice, but it's overtaken by anger. I start to shove people out of my way when they refuse to move. The crowd continues enlarging, but I hear a faint voice command, "Everybody move."

The mob splits in half, leaving me looking down a narrow path. At the end of the path stands President Atrox. His skin is paler in the sunlight.

Despite the paleness of his skin, small portions of his cheeks are rosy. It's probably makeup for the cameras.

"Let Ms. Kingston through peacefully."

Everybody stands silent for a few seconds, before I realize that I'm supposed to walk through. I begin marching through the opening—trying to take even strides.

I reach President Atrox shortly, and his arm encases my shoulders as I'm led forward. He appears to be guiding me, but it feels like he's dragging me along.

He pulls me all the way up the marble steps, and through the huge doors. When we get inside, he releases me and says, "Don't fail me today, Alice. Remember that Amica can be put back in her rightful position as easily as she was removed from it."

I glare at him, seemingly locked in his frozen stare. A thought crosses my mind and I say it without thinking, "If you put her back, wouldn't the other slaves question how she was freed then enslaved again?"

He grins slightly, revealing his crooked teeth. He nods as if he's considering what I've said, "That is true," While he's talking, I instantly regret asking him this. There's only one other option for him, "I guess I'd just have to kill her instead."

His words echo through the marble hall. Nothing absorbs his words, so it repeats many times. *I guess I'd just have to kill her instead.*

I feel the color drain from my face. Why would I ask that? How did I not see what he would say?

His grin grows to a wicked smile as he begins walking away. I stand solid, feet planted into the ground. It feels like I can't move. I'm not entirely sure what to do; I can't exactly counter the president's offer.

"That wasn't the deal." I say, angrily.

He waves a dismissive hand—as though my thoughts are inferior. They are. Nothing I say could change his mind. About halfway through his walk, he glances back and says, "Auxillio will meet you in the drill room."

Chapter 11

ATROX DISAPPEARS FROM the great hall, and his words still ring within my mind. It's disturbing how he can get rid of people so easily. He's already thought about this. Maybe he wants to kill her, so he's waited until now to tell me.

During my walk to the drill room, my stomach twists. I scold myself for setting myself up like that. I should have been smarter. *Think before you act, Alice.*

President Atrox is truly insane. He's killed so many people, sent bombs to destroy the world, killed his own brother, and now is threatening to kill Amica! His brother was even more despicable than him, but the fact that he would kill his own flesh and blood, that's crazy.

I reach the drill room and I am let in by a single soldier. The room has black walls, and a white ceiling. One window occupies the far wall and is cracked open. It lets in a steady stream of fresh air.

It's refreshing to smell the fresh air. It almost makes me forget what's happened.

I've waited no more than five minutes, when Auxillio walks in looking anxious. The expression on her face changes when she sees me, "We must start right away, we're already ten minutes behind schedule."

I see a tear slide down her cheek, but I make no effort to comfort her. She hands me the speech cards and tells me to read. I read through the entire speech one time out loud. I estimate the length at around five minutes. She looks at me, and talks in a stressed tone, "I thought it would be longer." Another tear slides down her face, "We're just going to have to make do with what we have."

I nod and read it aloud again. As I finish the final few words, Mory and Nory walk in silently.

They interrupt my speaking, "Sorry we're late, not all of us have a private limo."

She was going to say more, but is cut off by Auxillio screaming, "In the hallway!"

Auxillio pulls them both outside the room swiftly. She meant to pull them out so I couldn't hear, but I can hear clearly enough.

"You can't be late! I don't want to fire you again!"

The Novus

It seems strange that she's fired them before. It sounded like they'd known each other forever and were great friends. Until now.

"Next time you're late, I'm firing you both, and..." She struggles, before concluding the thought, "Suing you!" I wonder if it's possible for her sue them for something so small. Nothing seems to be small to Auxillio.

She walks back into the room a few moments later, after more screaming and yelling. The expression on her face has cooled. Mory and Nory look as though they've survived a car wreck.

"Alright Alice, let's continue."

We run through the speech again, and I notice myself slowly becoming less dependent on the cards.

Over the next few hours, we read the speech many times. One time, Auxillio decides that my voice needs to sound more upbeat.

They attempt to coax me into it, but ultimately fail. Mory produces a voice modulator, and places it on my neck. It's a clear circular disk, that's no bigger than the tip of my thumb. It sticks to my neck, but I still feel it's presence. It bugs me. I itch it, and Mory warns me to stop. However, I can't seem to help it. Over and over, I continue to itch it. They don't catch me every time, but finally, Mory loses her temper and scolds me. I keep in mind that I shouldn't go too far with her.

Around ten, Auxillio decides that my performance is perfect, so we practice presenting. They tell me my body language is all wrong.

"You're just closed off," says Nory.

I stand for an hour while they move me around, getting every single detail correct.

By the end of it, my body is sore, and my bones creak when I move. It feels like I've lived a thousand years, and my body now pays the price.

They have me run through the speech a few times in my new position, and I'm relieved when Auxillio declares, "I think it's perfect. This calls for an early lunch."

I relax at the thought of food, and rush to the dining hall. I've been to the cafeteria with the Magna Council, but not the dining hall. I suppose it's for a higher level of dining within the Pura building.

The ceilings are higher, and the floors are marble once again. Tables sit far apart, each topped with beautiful napkins folded into flowers.

Auxillio and the twins walk in a few minutes after me. A slave finally arrives, and I order a simple grilled cheese with tomato soup. I'd consider it a delicacy, as my mother made it often before her death. I remember when I'd sit at the counter while it cooked on the pan. The cheese always extended into many strings and would get tangled around my tongue with every bite.

The Novus

Sometimes they would even make it for us in the refugee camps. However, food like that was scarce, and we hardly ever came across it.

When my food arrives, I wonder why it took twenty minutes to prepare. When I see it, I know exactly why? The bread is not typical pre-sliced bread. It appears to be an artisan loaf. The cheese is three different kinds, and each is either smoked, or spiced.

The tomato soup steams and is a dull red color. The dull red is interrupted by floating spices, and crumbled crackers. The meal itself tastes great but lacks the charm of my mother's.

I swallow my feelings because I'm starving. As I eat it, I watch Auxillio, and her assistants eat as well. They couldn't afford extra food other than the visitor's package—which consists of a ham and cheese sandwich, along with an apple. I had offered to buy them something extra, but they declined.

When we all finish our meals, it's around noon. We have one hour left until the speech. Auxillio guides me from the dining hall to a dressing room. The room is made of unevenly arranged white marble bricks. The cracks are filled with golden lines of cement.

The room is designed in a symmetrical radial pattern, each wing leading into a short hallway or changing room.

The ceiling gathers at the top, extending into a cone like shape. At the top, it cuts off, and becomes a sky light. The sky light is artificial. It's only an illusion. It's how the Pura building has so many different shaped rooms, while the entire structure is uniform on the outside.

Auxillio has me stand in the center, directly beneath the skylight. She runs off into a different section and comes back wheeling in a cart.

On the cart is a singular hanger, occupied by a tall plastic bag, "This..." She pauses to lick her lips, "Cost quite a bit. One of the most expensive dresses left in Pura."

"Why would I wear a fancy dress? Wouldn't that make people less receptive of my speech?"

"You'd think, but the president insisted that you wear a dress. All he said was that he had his reasons."

"Why is it so expensive?"

"Well, it's vintage. From the styles of before the war."

I nod, and realize it makes sense. After the war, most clothing styles died out, and were taken up by Pura City's boring attire. Almost all clothes are navy blue and gold now, but any others are simply gray or black—with the exception of Auxillio's strange clothing choices.

Fashionable clothes from before the war grew in price. It's a dying breed, but they're preserved by a few designers in the city, and apparently Malus town as well.

While reorganizing my thoughts, I watch Auxillio pull the dress off the rack.

She sets it on a nearby table and unzips the plastic. Inside is a light blue dress with a golden belt. The rest fades into a darker blue in the lower section, and the entire thing is trimmed with gold.

"Go try it on." She smiles as she says this—as though I care about the dress. I move to a dressing room. Five minutes later—after I figured out how to operate the dress—I exit the dressing room, and my steps are followed by a squeal from Auxillio, "Don't you just love it?"

I nod, but now that I'm wearing it, the dress feels distant. In a mirror, I see my face on top of the dress. It feels like somebody else is wearing it. Somebody more deserving.

With less than twenty minutes left before my speech, we all run to the Presidential office.

When we reach the office, I'm once again amazed by the beauty of the room. The flowing waterfalls, dazzling diamonds, and golden plates all decorate the extraordinary room.

I'm brought back to reality by the one thing that makes the room ugly. President Atrox. He sits at his desk, shuffling papers—as though other people don't do his busy work for him.

He looks up and greets us with a friendly smile. I suspect that only I can see right through it. I never noticed that his smile is extremely tall and shows his gums.

I ponder the subject some more and realize that he's gotten plastic surgery. It's not uncommon in Pura City, because people claim it makes the city better. In President Atrox's case, it just adds to the list of things about him that make me sick.

I think about how he's changed over the years. He used to be tanner, but they probably made him paler to seem older. To seem wiser.

His eyes have grown, and now his mouth is bigger as well. Why change everything about him except for the many wrinkles that too obviously display the changes on his face?

I can see a crease where they tucked in the sagging skin, and I notice a subtle line above his mouth where they attached the taller lip.

It makes me sad to realize that all these changes were to make him look older, wiser, and nicer. It makes him look disturbingly ugly.

I force myself to stop thinking about Atrox's plastic surgery, because I don't have much time left before my speech.

"Welcome everybody, the Presidential balcony is behind me. That is where Alice will stand. People have been gathering for the past hour," says Atrox.

I still quake in his presence. I've become a public figure with high authority, but I feel like I'm still watching him on television.

The Novus

"Alright Alice, come on over." Auxillio gestures me over while saying this.

She swipes hair out of my eyes and reminds me to speak into the microphone. She must notice color leaving my face, because she goes on, "Alice, remember. You are the best!"

Her voice lacks in no department, but I fear that mine will, "Two minutes until showtime," says Nory.

The thought of Amica's fate hardly crosses my mind, because somehow, I'm more occupied with being nervous about speaking in front of thousands of people.

People gather inside the office. Most are government employees. I notice Eli standing in line with the former Magna. Somehow his presence makes the experience seem less intimidating.

Lapis and Alium accompany his sides, but they stand in a way that almost ignores my presence. I see the new Magna Council standing across the room, most of them ignoring me as well. Although I notice Conso staring me down. We lock eyes for a moment, and it feels like the whole world freezes. It feels like she's trying to make everything worse.

It feels like I'll throw up but I force myself to stop. I can't. I won't.

Mory warns me, "One minute!"

Everybody is running around the office frantically, making sure everything will be perfect.

"Citizens are still trying to get into the viewing area!"

"Will the mic be loud enough?"

All of the screaming chatter is broken up when President Atrox says, "Enough! She's fine," He makes sure to lock his eyes on mine for the last part, "It will be *perfect*."

It has to be perfect, or else Amica is done.

Auxillio slams her hand onto my back and guides me into the archway that leads to the balcony. Immediately, I see a camera with a small blinking red light. The broadcast has begun.

I swallow, feeling a lump in the back of my throat. With each step I take, the lump grows. I feel like I'll fall over the white marble railing, but I tell myself to pull it all together. I do my best to collect my feelings.

As I reach the railing, I realize that I couldn't have prepared for this. Thousands upon thousands of people occupy the streets. Each one watching intently. Watching me.

I think about my mother. What would she think about me right now? Would she despise me for standing up for the city? Would she love me for protecting a friend? I do know that she would have found a better way to do it. She was very intuitive.

I search the crowds for Amica but know that it's ridiculous. I'm too high up to even see anybody's face—not to mention that there are thousands of people out there.

I glance behind me and see Auxillio nodding her head. It's time to go.

Chapter 12

I LOOK BACK out to the audience—wondering what all these people think of me.

My eyes focus on looking forward. It's difficult due to two cameras that lay only a few feet away from me.

I smile while looking out to the audience. It feels like the time is dragging on, and I suddenly remember that I need to start, "Welcome, citizens of Pura City. We thank you for taking time out of your day to listen.

"We gather, due to the unrest in our society. Protests, and riots spread throughout the city, all because of a misunderstanding.

"We've endured war, bombs, and just as we thought we would die, we pulled through and survived. We collected the remains of our society and formed a city that vowed to never see another war ever again.

"We purified humanity in hopes of eliminating all evil. The crime rate has dropped to almost zero. We're at our peak, only for it to be destroyed by a misinterpretation."

My eyes focus back on the camera. It's disturbing to know that so many people are watching me right now. What are they thinking? Do they like it? The words seem to flow out of my mouth all on their own, and there's no meaning behind it.

"It is understood by city leaders that some think it's unfair to enslave low scoring students. The low scoring students should be willing to sacrifice themselves. In fact, I believe that anybody should be willing to sacrifice themselves for the greater good of humanity.

"Don't think of it as becoming a slave to society, or a prisoner to a test. Think of it as becoming a hero. All the low scoring students are heroes. You are all saving humanity. I'm not sure we could thank you enough but take this speech as a thank you. We thank you for saving us, our children, and the generations to come."

The speech doesn't stop there. I realize that I've talked too fast and need to fill the remaining time. I basically restate what I've already said in a different format. The words don't exactly add much value to the speech.

I finally finish with, "So, thank you for saving us, all. It's thanks to all the low scoring students, that Pura City will last forever!"

My voice quiets, and I realize that the extra bit has added no more than one minute to the speech. and I wait for the audience to react. They're silent. I feel as though I've been standing here for hours when the audience bursts into applause.

I smile, but it slowly fades as I realize who is actually clapping. It's clear that the better dressed people are the average scoring citizens. The protester's clothes look as though they've been wearing them for days.

There's no applause from the slaves, or protesters. They stand silently, with looks of anger displayed on their faces. I find it difficult to lie to myself. I can't deny that most of the citizens are quiet as well.

My chin raises, and I try to bring the smile back. It comes, but only halfway. The camera in front of me stops blinking, so I know the broadcast has ended.

I spin around slowly, careful to not trip. I walk back into Atrox's office, hoping that he's miraculously disappeared. I shrug when I see him walking directly towards me.

He walks up to me and leans in close. His breath lightly grazes my face, but it smells horrible. *Like death.*

Finally, he whispers, "Not good enough."

My breathing accelerates in pace as he says this. I watch him smirk, knowing he attained the desired effect. He reaches in for a hug, to make the entire thing seem sincere to the outside world. I gently push him away and walk towards Auxillio.

"Alice, you did great! Some of the protesters stopped screaming!" She displays a huge toothy smile. I try to return a smile, but it comes out looking pathetic.

I glance towards Eli, who's firm position has broken, and he walks towards me slowly, "The speech was perfect, Alice. You're doing Pura a great favor."

I blush as Auxillio pulls me away. She guides me to the door, and right when we're about to leave, the president says, "Everybody leave. Except for Ms. Kingston."

He grins as I gulp nervously. He manages to make me feel so powerless. Auxillio and the others leave. President Atrox and I stand in the middle of the Presidential office. Alone.

"Alice, sit."

He's not asking. I sit in the seat before his desk, while he sits in his, "That was very moving Ms. Kingston."

"Thank you."

"Let me finish," He rubs his hand over his graying hair, and asks, "What did you think of the crowd's reaction."

I think, although I already know my answer, "They applauded."

"Who?"

I hesitate, "The citizens."

"And who wasn't applauding?"

I know the answer, I've known it from the start. It wasn't difficult to predict the outcome, but it almost seems like Atrox was hoping for it. Odd.

"The slaves."

"The speech was to calm the slaves. And yet here we are. You've gotten nowhere."

His bottom lip drops, revealing a small gap between his lips. A dark void lies behind it, waiting to release his next argument. I feel myself shrinking into the depths of my chair.

He looks at me, as though he expects me to say something. So, I do, "Sir, you have to know even better than me that it will take more than one speech to convince these people."

"You're absolutely right." I'm put at ease for a brief second before he continues, "It will take two speeches."

My bones tighten, and I clench my jaw, "But sir, that is impossible to—"

He cuts me off, "You have one more chance," he holds up his hand—indicating for me to stop talking, "If you fail, then Amica will die."

I leave immediately after he said that. Auxillio escorts me out of the building, asking what he talked to me about. I tell her to silence herself.

We make our way down the staircase, when reporters bombard me yet again.

"Do you really think the slaves should sacrifice themselves?"

"Are you saying that the citizens of Pura City aren't smart for misunderstanding the system?"

I walk through, attempting to push my way out of the crowd. They spit questions into my ear, and they all put words into my mouth. I can't even remember what I truly said. The filler part at the end was a blur, and the entire experience was chaotic.

They all surround me, and all I can hear is their voices speaking into their microphones. It gets to the point where it's so loud, so I cover my ears. My eyes close, and I hold my breath—as if it will make them go away.

Then, a sound even louder than the reporters breaks into the shield I made with my hands. A gunshot. It's crisp, and precise.

My eyes dart frantically in all directions, searching for the source. Most people fall to the ground, and I follow swiftly.

Another shot goes off no more than five feet in front of my face.

It's difficult to separate the sounds. Screaming reporters, barking soldiers, and crying children. More gunshots ring out, and I identify the source to my left.

A small man with golden hair holds a small gun, and he's pointing it towards me. My body recoils at the sensation, but something powerful pulls him away. I watch him fall to the ground, unconscious.

A soldier replaces his position, and drags me from the ground, "Ms. Kingston, we must leave immediately."

He drags me the whole way there. Gunshots shoot closer towards us, and I hear the soldier cry out in pain as one pierces into his thick boot.

I'm relieved as he practically throws me into the limo and climbs in behind me. The door slams shut. I examine the large soldier. Broad shoulders, thick gloves, sunglasses, and a golden pauldron. On his pauldron is a Pura flower, with golden bumps surrounding it. I identify him as a Pura building guard. More specifically, a military specialist.

He barks orders to the driver, "We need to get to the Presidential circle fast."

It's not Ordell.

The driver nods and begins to accelerate. He reaches high speeds—probably to the limo's limit. I can't help but feel sick. From the gunshots—that still explode outside the limo—to Atrox, to Amica. Everything is falling apart.

We race past blurred images, and then a bullet bursts through the window. I duck my head, and then the soldier's walkie-talkie says in a muffled voice, "Military vehicles are closing in on the city circle."

How did the protesters get a hold of guns?

The soldier clenches his fist in frustration and tells the driver to drive as fast as possible. He slams the gas harder and I'm jolted forward. I realize that once the military vehicles trap the protesters, we'll be trapped as well.

Another bullet shatters the window on the soldier's side. His face goes red, and he looks infuriated at this point. He reaches to his belt and pulls out a small handgun.

I don't register his actions until he aims it out the shattered window, "Stop!" I scream.

I instinctively climb from my seat and slide down the row of seats until I reach him. My wrist wraps around his arm, and I attempt to pull it down. He must be three times my size, because he doesn't even budge.

He shoots three times, and the noise is deafening. I scream yet again and hope to annoy him at this point. I'm screaming directly into his ear, and he finally shoves me out of the way. I fall to the floor of the limo, and my head bangs against the ground.

A nauseating pain fills my head, but I'm determined to keep going. I begin to get up, but the car screeches to a halt. My head jumps forward, and bangs against the base of a seat. The driver yells back, "The military vehicles have closed in!"

The soldier ignores him, but I can tell he's frustrated. I hoist myself from the ground and look out the broken window. The first thing I see is soldiers shooting through the crowds.

Chapter 13

SOLDIERS POUR OUT of huge trucks, closing in on the protesters. Only a few protesters hold guns. The rest stand there defenseless. I throw the door open, but it appears to be jammed.

I manage to create a small hole, and squeeze through it. My foot gets stuck in the end, and I feel the soldier grab my foot, "Get back in!"

I slip my arm back through the hole and pry his fingers from my shoe. It's no easy task, and I think I may have broken one of his fingers. I grit my teeth and move on.

I run through the road screaming, "Stop shooting! Stop!"

My voice cracks halfway through and is covered in sobs. I continue running and set my gaze on the first soldier I can focus on.

She's still fifteen yards away, when I see her shoot down a young man. His lifeless body falls to the floor, and my anger grows. She shot down the boy so easily, but I know I can't direct my anger towards her. *It's Atrox's fault. Everything is Atrox's fault.*

It doesn't matter if it's Atrox's fault. That woman still chose to shoot that young man, and she will pay the price.

I sprint faster, and when I reach her, I direct my elbow into her shoulder. I lack fighting experience but continue anyways.

I'm taller than her, so I easily reach her shoulder, but she's still stronger. I wrestle her for her gun, but she doesn't budge. I attempt using my elbow again, but she shoves me to the ground in one swift motion. My body lands with a twist and a snap. My arm took the worst of the fall. I think it's broken.

My eyes dart towards the horror, and notice that my elbow is inverted. Blood spills from a scrape that I received on the pavement. For a moment, I feel distant, and imagine what I look like to others. *A young girl, covered in blood, fighting for a gun.*

I shift myself back to the reality where I'm lying on the road, helplessly trying to defend the protesters. *The protesters who started this attack. Against me.*

I can't blame them. I would be a part of these riots as well if I wasn't on the Magna Council. Well, maybe not me, but Amica definitely would.

My mind starts to drift, and the world is twisting. I try to focus on the soldier that broke my arm, but I can't seem to find her. I search in all directions, but no matter where I look, the world still spins.

I feel a faint prick in my neck, and everything spins faster. All the surroundings begin blurring together. The noise from the gunshots swirl into screams, and everything seems to fold up, into darkness.

I feel myself awaken, although I can't see anything but darkness. I can move my eyes under my eyelids. I feel my body but can't move it.

A tiny voice says, "If I give her the Silno vitamin, than she'll get her movement back by the time she wakes up."

I find myself able to open my eyes but keep them closed to listen. I wonder if they can detect that I'm awake.

"What about the other shot you talked about?" I recognize the voice as Amica's. I wonder why she's here. Where are we?

I ponder this thought some more as I drift back to sleep. I miss the conversation.

The sleep becomes darker, and eventually I can't feel anything.

My eyes pop open and I find tubes and wires connected to my arms and head. I'm in a white room with a hazy yellow feel to it.

To my left is a large box with monitors. Lines spike up and down but move at a rapid pace. Eventually, they all smooth to a steady up and down spike.

Holograms occupy a table in front of me, and I see a small lady standing over them. She drags green parts through the hologram, and gasps as she sees my open eyes.

"Oh! I didn't realize you were awake," She looks slightly worried, but replaces it with a smile, "I'll go grab your friend."

I realize that my *friend* is Amica. I was sure that Atrox killed Amica after my rebellious act at the battle.

I inspect the room some more as I wait, and peak at the hologram the nurse was working on. It's hard to see from my bed, but it looks like she was planning a surgery for me.

My arm is wrapped in a sling, and I try to imagine how much damage could have been done. I only fell and twisted it.

It was bleeding as well, but right now I feel no pain.

The Novus

The door swings open slowly, and I see Amica walking in. She walks to my bed and sits on a nearby stool.

She smiles, but her words don't match her expression, "You were supposed to be up two days ago!" She's almost yelling.

"Sorry?" My face squirms uncomfortably, and I watch waves of emotion fly across her face.

"Sorry, I've been here a while. They won't let me leave! You have to have a family member present for consultation, but since you have none, I had to stay to make your medical decisions."

I thank her for staying, and then we sit quietly. I realize the nurse is in the room as well, so I ask, "Will I need the surgery?"

"I thought so, but you seem to be fine. We'll do a simple heat treatment on your arm, and you'll be good as new by tomorrow."

"What's the heat treatment?" asks Amica.

"In simple terms, we numb her arm, and heat it. We can then mold the bone back into place."

I nod, and she knows it's approved by me. We go over the details and she has me sign a few papers. A bone specialist will be coming in an hour to complete the operation.

Over the next hour, Amica and I talk about the speech, "Alice, I'm not going to lie, it wasn't your best work."

She says it in a kind voice, I chuckle, "We really shouldn't be laughing about this. It's your life on the line."

She glares at me and says, "You need to stop worrying about me. At this point, forget about it. It's out of your hands."

I hope she knows that I won't stop worrying about her. If I fail, then she dies. It's simple, yet so complex.

"It's literally in my hands. I'm writing the speeches."

"But it will never be good enough. It's impossible to please everybody, and even more impossible to please yourself."

Her words make me think. I think about how Amica has grown from a teenager to a responsible adult in a matter of days. She's probably more stressed than I am. She wakes up every morning and wonders if I'll fail. If I fail, then she dies.

I ask Amica to leave, so I can nap before the bone specialist gets here. I don't fall asleep, but it feels nice to close my eyes.

Just as I feel myself drifting into sleep, the door opens; a really tall man walks in, "Hello, I'm Dr. Eko, head bone specialist in Pura City," I nod, and examine him. Probably in his forties. I notice a pen tucked behind his left ear—left-handed. His black hair is cut short, and his eyes are a flat brown, "Nurse Curri already told you about the operation, so I'm just going to proceed."

The Novus

He walks closer, and the closer he gets, the taller he becomes. He towers over me and casts a large shadow.

He's rather thin, and his hair looks brown instead of black now. I also notice a thin mustache resting upon his upper lip.

He slips on gloves with a fire logo on them—heat resistant, most likely—and grabs a box from the shelf. A thin square sits on the top, and he punches a code into it. The lid lifts automatically.

I can't quite see the contents, until he pulls out a strange compression sleeve with tubes strung around it.

He holds it with care, and walks over to me, "This is the heat sleeve. Don't worry about burn damage, you won't feel a thing."

I nod, and he slips it onto my arm carefully. It's easy to tell that he's experienced, because my arm doesn't hurt as he does this. The sleeve hugs my arm tightly, and the tubes all light up at once.

A slight burning sensation occurs, but it goes away almost instantly. My entire arm goes limp, and I can't feel anything. The tubes change to a bright orange color.

He props my arm on a rack, so he can work with it easier, "Alright, this will be done quick."

I gulp, nervously—unsure of what will happen—and he continues. One tube turns blue, and another turns green. He grabs the blue wire, and gently pulls it to the green wire. Somehow, they fuse together, and become one wire. It turns green.

The process starts again—one wire turns blue; the other wire turns green. They connect seamlessly, and I can feel the wires shifting my bone into the correct position. It's a strange operation and I wonder if there's an easier way to do it.

I watch the doctor, who's brow is sweating, yet his hands don't shake. I'm relieved when all of the wires are green, and he turns a small dial at the end of the sleeve. Strangely, I can feel my bone hardening.

He removes the sleeve shortly after, and carefully places it back into the box.

I inspect my arm, and watch as he gets up to wash his hands, "How's it feel?"

I stop to think. I move it slightly—scared that it will hurt—and find that it doesn't hurt at all, "It feels great. That's incredible."

"It really is," he walks over to the table, and begins shuffling through papers, "It's hard to believe there was a time when it took weeks to fix broken bones."

I nod. They had all the technology; they just didn't know how to use it.

"I'll send Nurse Curri back in a second."

He leaves shortly after, and Nurse Curri walks in behind him, "How'd it go?"

"Great, I feel good."

The Novus

She walks over to a table and grabs a few more papers. Then, she pulls the wires off my head and arms.

With my ability to move around once again, I immediately get up and follow her to the table. She's laid out a few papers. I quickly take a pen, sign them, and she allows me to leave. My status paid for the visit.

I call for my limo, and it arrives shortly after. While I climb into the back, the driver begins driving quickly. I'm flung inside the car, and I fall to the floor, "Sorry about that." apologizes the driver.

I try to pull myself up, but find it difficult, "Why are you driving so fast?"

He sighs while I ask, "Just in case if any protesters are around," he glances in the mirror and watches me struggle to get up, "Sorry."

I grit my teeth, and finally work up the strength to hoist myself off the ground. I find that we're pulling into the Presidential circle when I peer out the window. From here, I can see my house still glowing. It truly is a beautiful sight, and I wish I could appreciate it more. He finally pulls up to the curb before my house and—as I get out—I notice President Atrox walking up the steps.

My mind immediately turns in many different directions. What's he doing here? I quietly climb back into the limo, and order the driver to wait until he leaves, "Ms. Kingston, I got to put the limo back for charging."

There's nothing I can do about it. I push open the heavy door and climb out silently—trying to not draw attention to myself. I fail, however, and Atrox calls to me from the platform, "Alice, won't you join me?"

His eyes are far away, but I can still see the satisfaction within them. He wants me to lose. He wants to kill Amica. But why? And why would he drag me on like this, if he knew he would kill her to begin with?

I walk up the stairs quickly—eager to end the encounter, "What do you need?" My words come out in an irritated tone, and I watch him recoil. He's not used to being disrespected.

"I just wanted to check on you. Make sure that your... priorities are correct."

My mind picks up on the word *wanted*. It was a direct response to me saying *need*. He's reminding me that he can do whatever he wants. He's clever. It's these small details that he plants into my mind. It all causes strange emotions, and he ultimately triumphs.

"What priorities?" I ask, trying to hide the truth. I know the truth, and he obviously does as well.

"Well truly, if you were loyal to our system, then writing a good speech would be easy. Correct?"

I nod.

"So, in theory, writing a good speech would mean that you believed in our system. If you wrote a bad speech, then you must not be—"

I cut him off before he can expose me, "Sir, I am loyal to Pura City. But it's difficult to write a speech that satisfies everybody's needs." I think back to when Amica said that earlier.

He holds my gaze with his and seems to be searching for the truth. I'm not sure how to lie effectively, and certainly not as well as Atrox. He definitely has experience in that field.

"Of course, it's difficult. I've tried myself. But it's a certain tone in your voice. Not to mention our previous conversations where you've unknowingly told me the real answer to this question."

Is this true? Have I told him? I try to counter his argument, "Sir, as you've said though, you've tried speeches yourself. If they haven't worked, then doesn't that mean that you aren't loyal to Pura?"

I mentally slap myself in the face. Why would I say that?

"Are you suggesting that I don't support my own city? That I simply do this system to enslave my citizens? I don't want slaves, but it's absolutely necessary to restore order in our world!" His pale face is beginning to redden, and I scold myself for causing it.

"No sir. I'm sure you would never do that for the satisfaction of slavery. A smart leader has a reason for everything. I'm sure you have yours, because you're certainly smart." I can feel the conversation's tension easing, and his face becomes bone white once again.

His head leans in towards mine, and he whispers, "I hope that your priorities are in the right place, Alice. Remember, if they're not, then Amica dies."

He rushes down the steps immediately after, before I even get a chance to think about his words. He's right. If I'm not loyal to Pura, then I can't make good speeches. And if I can't make good speeches, then Amica dies.

The thought is like sealing an envelope. It's done. I'm not loyal to Pura, so Amica will die.

I didn't sleep that night and woke up the next morning feeling pathetic. The last thing I thought last night wasn't even about Amica. Right before I feel asleep, I muttered the word *failure*.

I'm not sure why I thought that word. Probably because of the failed speech. The failed attempt to stop the soldiers. Especially my failed attempt to save Amica.

I feel pathetic. I've become scared of an old man and can't protect my own friend. When I woke up this morning, I felt more tired than normal. It agitates me due to the fact that I have Magna Council duties today.

I pull myself out of bed and get ready quickly. It doesn't take me long to slip out of the mansion, and into the limo. When I get in, I notice that the driver is the same as the original. Ordell.

He begins driving slowly, and I notice him subtly avoiding my eyes. It's easy to tell that he's not in a talkative mood, but I need answers. I run through the list, and stop on the most logical one I find, "Ordell, why do my drivers keep switching?"

We come upon a red light, and he stops abruptly, "No reason."

I can easily detect that there's more to the story. I note that I only have so long before he closes off completely, "Well, it just seemed odd that it takes more than one person to drive for me," I realize that my argument isn't substantial, so I think about all of our conversations. As I examine the rearview mirror, I notice that Ordell's uniform has one simple design. A small Pura flower with a golden circle around it. It's simplistic, but it still sparks a memory of the other driver's uniform. His was a Pura flower as well, but I clearly remember a silver circle around it. It seems insignificant, but it must relate to rank, "Not to mention that the other drivers are substitutes."

The thought comes out of my mouth smoothly. Gold is surely above silver rank, and there can't be many ranks when it comes to drivers. The others have to be substitutes.

I examine his expression. He sighs, and the corners of his mouth curl up as he speaks, "You're very perceptive, aren't you?" He pauses, as if he's contemplating what's safe to share with me. *He is hiding something*, "But you're right. The others are substitutes. Sometimes I have more... important issues to deal with."

I wonder why he pauses before saying *important issues*. Perhaps he's hiding something huge. He knew Auxillio, so maybe he's against Pura. If he is, then why is he a driver?

I decide to not press any further, because I get the feeling that if I press too far, it will make him hide. Ordell is a very secretive person, and I don't want to scare him off.

Chapter 14

ORDELL DROPS ME off at the Pura building, and I walk in quickly. I'm happy to see no reporters, and no protesters. The soldiers must have scared them off. I walk straight through the halls, and into the Magna room. Everybody has already arrived.

When I walk in, they all fall silent. I wonder why, until I realize that I've missed a lot of Magna Council days. They've been working together, and now I'm the outsider.

I stand silently, until I finally say, "What'd I miss?"

Conso glares at me, "You missed quite a bit. Where've you been?"

"In the hospital," I reply, hastily, "I was attacked after my speech."

"Big surprise..." mutters Zed, trailing off.

"Well, thankfully you didn't miss too much. We just made a few minor decisions," says Nita—who is much nicer than the others.

"We finished our apprenticeship. The mentors are gone, but Oraculi volunteered to teach you the rest," says Avetay.

I'm not sure how to react, but I feel my face go red. Is this connected to his request for me to call him Eli?

The conversation seems to stop on its own, and Nita continues, "We heard about the mob attacking you, but they didn't give us that much information." I thank Nita, and we get to work. I feel behind even before we open the folder in front of us. The way they all so swiftly flip it open makes me feel like I've missed so much. Before I get a chance to read it mentally, Avetay reads aloud.

It's about a group of stragglers found in the eastern section of the world. A city representative analyzed the situation and declared that they're not a part of any colony—although I find it unfair because they were only two miles away from the nearest one. Anyways, it's a group of teenage boys, along with a few adults.

The theory is that they were a camping group who got stranded during the war. Given their survival skills, they survived in the wild. Zed is the first to speak, "It's simple, there's hardly a decision to make. We pick them up by helicopter and bring them back."

"And if they're over eighteen then we'll give them the test." Adds Conso.

I watch Zane wince as I glance towards him. Specifically, when Conso says the word *test*. As though he's not a fan of it—like most people.

Zane looks like he's trying to hold in his anger, "But what if they don't want to come to Pura City? What if they don't want to take the test?"

"They don't really have a choice," snaps Conso.

"I guess that's the decision we have to make" I say. Everybody pauses to stare at me. *I am the outsider.* So, I continue, "Should we bring them back and make them take the test, or not?"

"Ms. Kingston is correct," says a voice near the entrance of the room. President Atrox. His skin looks less pale in the dim lighting, "Should we bring them back? Or not?"

"Wouldn't *you* want to bring them back?" asks Zane. He should be more careful. It's too obvious that he's against Pura City.

Atrox chuckles before responding, "Well I want to, but this is out of my *legal* jurisdiction. Technically I can overrule any law, but this one is typically done by the Magna. Besides, it doesn't really concern me."

He doesn't *overrule* the law. He breaks it. Although nobody would ever say that. Unless if they have a dying wish.

Over the next few minutes, we debate the topic. I side with bringing them back—but only to side with President Atrox. I need to gain his trust. If I don't, then Amica dies. At least his standards are very clear towards me.

Zed, Conso, and I all side with bringing them back. Nita, Avetay, and Zane all protest by saying we shouldn't. I begin to wonder if President Atrox is testing my loyalty with this decision. I also wonder if he can tell that I don't actually side with them.

"Why don't we just ask them if they want to come back?" proposes Zane. I shrug as he says this. After a few minutes of discussion, he's run out of arguments, and now these people will come to Pura City.

"That would be undermining the Magna Council's authority. Not to mention that if the citizens found out, they would be furious that they're forced to take the test, while others aren't." Counters Conso.

That is the deciding factor, "Then it's settled. We'll pick them up tomorrow by helicopter," concludes Atrox.

We all nod, and I try to make mine look sincere, "That's all you're needed for today," says the president.

The Novus

We all get up to leave, but Atrox asks me to hang back for a second, "What do you need?" I ask, trying to sound kind—although I sense that he can detect my uneasiness.

He seems to think about his answer before responding—which is odd, because he always knows what he's going to say.

"I'd love for you to stop by the Pura building study. It's a library as well. Perhaps you could pick up a book on writing speeches."

I purse my lips as he says this. He knows very well that I tried as hard as I could, because it's to save my friend's life. He's downplaying my abilities.

Either way, I have no choice, so I leave. I'm not sure where the study is, so I wander around the second floor first. I notice Eli walking down the hall on the opposite side, so I make my way over.

I intended to ask him where the study is, but my words lean into a different direction, "What are you doing here?"

He's only a few feet away when he responds, "Even though I'm no longer a part of the Magna, they've given me a spot on the government," he begins. I wonder if by *given* he actually means forced, "I scored almost as high as you, Alice."

This fact piques my interest. I know he was the first to be accepted into the Magna affiliate's program, but I don't remember what his score was when they broadcasted it last year. I'm struggling to remember, so I ask, "What was your score?"

His face goes red, and I can tell I've crossed a line. It must be a sensitive topic for him. It certainly is for me, "A score doesn't matter, Ms. Kingston. It doesn't define who we are."

I feel my body shrink as he says this. He resumes his track down the hall, and I resume mine. The conversation was strange, and I begin thinking about it more as time drags on. Why is it a sensitive topic for him? I don't like Pura City, and the system is practically killing my best friend. Has something like that happened to him?

I'm not sure, and the thoughts stop when I come upon a large door. *Study.* How lucky is that? The door is pushed open by guards, and I walk in. The room is very different from the others. The walls are a dark wood, and the floor is hardwood as well. Portraits of President Atrox and other important figures line the walls. Desks are lined up, along with blue seats. A reception desk sits in one of the corners, with no person behind it.

Around the perimeter of most of the walls, are bookshelves. Thick and thin books are placed carefully on each shelf. It's a massive collection. Some of the shelves are bent from time, and others look brand new.

I walk towards the reception desk. There's no worker behind it, so I open one of the computers on my own. A catalog webpage shows up, and I search for public speaking. A card is automatically printed, and I pick it up. There are only three books on public speaking. The card doesn't display the titles, but it displays the section.

I navigate through the large study and come upon the correct shelf. This shelf is one of the older ones, yet I still find the books immediately. They sit together, side by side. I read each title carefully. *Public Speaking 101: By Anita Trineson.* The next is, *How to Speak, publicly: By Jeanette Carson.* The third book is titled *A Long guidE to publiC speakIng.*

The title is odd, and it has no author. I'm confused by the odd choice of capitalization. I slip it off the shelf and walk over to one of the desks. While I examine the cover, I notice the pattern. My brain runs through the most logical process it can.

All the words that should be capitalized aren't. Except for *A, and Long.* The letters that are capitalized are in odd places of each word. Perhaps it's some type of code about the book. It seems fun. My mother used to give me word unscramblers in the refugee camps.

So, if my logic is correct, then the letters I need are *A, L, E, C,* and *I.* The second I think about these letters alone, I already know what it is. *Alice.* I'm not even sure if there are other combinations, but this can't be a coincidence. I flip open the cover, and immediately begin looking for an author. No luck. I search the inside cover, and the back. Then, I search the first few pages. It would be wasteful to read the entire book. It's probably eight-hundred pages long.

Instead, I continue reading the next few pages. I guess Atrox told me to read one anyways. This way, I'll get to do both.

I read the table of contents, so I don't waste my time:

Before I finish reading, I already know the hidden message. *Kingston.* In which case, the full message is *Alice Kingston.* My name, but why is it there? What do I do now? It seems illogical that I would have to read the entire book to find the last answer.

There's not much more I can do except think. The message is my name. Perhaps it's a key. Maybe a password, or maybe the message goes on throughout the book. I pick up all the pages and thumb them down in a cascading wave—as if it will help my problem. It kind of does because it gives me an idea. While the pages pour down, a library card falls out. It's like the one I got from the computer. *The computer.*

I rush over immediately. It's still logged in, and I'm glad to see the receptionist is still gone. I type into the search bar, *Alice Kingston*. It loads slowly, and finally a short message pops up. *One result.* Below the message, is an image of a book cover. It's simply a dark brown background with the text, *Kristene.*

My mind stops racing. Kristene is my mother's name. This is no longer any type of coincidence. Even my inner skeptic can't deny this.

I print out the card immediately and run to the other end of the library. It's near a corner, and it looks like nobody's ever gotten a book from this shelf. The two shelves running into the corner are different. One is full of books, and the other is completely empty—which seems odd. I find the brown book tucked between two bright red novels on the filled shelf. It's obvious that it's been hidden on purpose. The brown cover matches the shelf, and it looks like a gap in between the red novels.

As I'm about to grab it, I stop myself. What will happen? I feel like I'm being ridiculous, but something tells me that Atrox wanted me to find this. *He sent me here.* I know for a fact that he doesn't want to kill me, and if he did, it wouldn't be in the

Pura building. It would be somewhere else, so he could easily frame somebody other than himself.

So, I ignore my doubts, and grab the book. It takes me a second to grip it—since it's so thin—but when I do, a quiet screeching noise occurs. It's very quiet, but it's definitely there. I search for the sound and it's easier than I expected. All I had to do was look towards the empty shelf, where each section is folding over. Now, the empty shelf has no sections.

Nothing else happens and I'm confused. Is that it? This entire journey led to a shelf that gets rid of each section. As I inspect closer, I notice a short brown knob emerging from the wooden wall. A door. A secret door.

It leads to a secret room. The thought thrills me. I always found secret rooms fascinating, however daunting they may seem. Why is there a secret room in the Pura building? The Pura building is full of secrets.

I finally work up the courage to turn the knob. It's not very old, so this door was probably put in two to four years ago. When the door is open, the gap is smaller than expected.

I step through slowly, and the room is dark. Pitch black. I release my grip on the door, but it springs shut. Shortly after, the quiet screeching occurs, and I'm afraid that I might be trapped. *Don't jump to conclusions, Alice. Yet.*

The Novus

It seems odd to me that I'm not scared of being trapped in here. I'm sure that I'll stay alive. Atrox doesn't want to kill me. He wants to see my pain when he kills Amica. All of these thoughts reassure me, so I step in more.

I'm not exactly sure how big the room is. I can't see any more than five feet in front of me, but I can sense that there's more than that.

It's awfully silent, and the only thing I can hear is my breathing. At the thought of my breathing, I find it difficult to maintain a steady pattern. It starts to become unsteady—as if I have to control it manually.

My feet creep forward silently, moving into the room slowly. As I advance into the room, a wall comes into view. It's painted a dark gray, but that's not what concerns me. Hanging on the wall is a portrait. I stare at it, and it takes me a second to recognize the person in the image. I haven't seen the face in so long. It's my mother.

Chapter 15

I ALMOST SCREAM, but I force myself to stay controlled. I'm not sure why I'm so surprised. What did I expect? The clues were obviously connected to my mother and myself.

It's still strange. I examine the portrait some more. First, I wonder why my mother is painted—she certainly couldn't afford a portrait. Second, I wonder why it's in a secret room in the government building.

The image is well painted, and I notice a faded signature at the bottom. The signature is the initials *OD,* written in curly loops.

I focus back on my mother. She wears a dull pink and blue coat, with a raggedy, old feel to it. Other than the robe, my mother is anything but aged. Her face appears to be younger than I ever saw her. Clean of wrinkles, and her hair no longer has a gray streak near the part.

The background is a very dark brown void, swirling in a circular motion. I can't help but wonder what the painting is about.

I glance down for only a second and notice an envelope sitting on a short table below my waist. The envelope is closed with a stamped seal. The Pura flower seal.

The envelope appears to be a few years old, and the seal is so dry that it peels off the envelope when I lift it.

I slide it off and open the flap. My fingers prop it open while I carefully slide out the contents. The contents are a smaller envelope, along with some folded medical records.

I decide to examine the envelope first. I open it carefully and pull out a folded letter. The writing is done in neat handwriting, and it says:

10/4/77

Dear future Alice,

You won't read this for another few years, but you need to know what's happening. Unfortunately, I can't tell you everything, but I can at least tell you what's going on.

I'm sorry that you must be monitored so closely by the president. It's because he sees you as a threat. You have a rare disorder called Mutated Cerebrum. It's not a disorder though. It's an advantage. Your brain runs at faster speeds, and your logic is greater than most.

President Atrox knows about it. He feels threatened. Anybody with M.C. could easily surpass him in any department.

Before I continue to read, I stop to let the words sink in. If I can easily surpass him in any department, then how has he manipulated me so easily?

He wanted you dead. It was the only way to stop you; but I offered an alternative. I gave myself to him, and he agreed to kill me instead. Killing me would disorient you enough so that you can't possibly apply your smarts.

However, you had a friend. I hope you're still friends with her. Your life depends on it. I suspect that he'll find out about your friend. He will do anything short of killing you.

I'm currently sitting in a cell awaiting my death. Don't worry about me. I've accepted it, because it's for you. I'm sending this letter with Odie; he has a place for it in the Pura building.

Just stay safe Alice. I don't know if Atrox is close to you, but if you're reading this in the Pura building right now, then I assume you're already close to him.

Love,
Mom

I hold back a tear as I set down the letter. My mind scans through it one more time to make sure I read it right. I did.

My mother's death wasn't an unidentified disease. I can't believe I didn't see it before. How could I think she just dropped dead from an ancient disease?

My mother died because of me. I killed her, not Atrox.

I bang my fist on the table in frustration. I almost have all the answers, but it's still not enough. This letter leaves me wanting more. So, I move towards the medical records. As I read through them, I realize they just talk about M.C.— as my mother called it.

I stuff the records into my pocket, along with the letter. Then something bugs me. Why would Atrox lead me here? Me finding this gives me leverage against him in our continuous battle. He can't confuse me anymore. Probably.

My stomach churns as I think about it. I run through the letter one more time, and see something new, "Who's Odie?" I mutter.

A quiet screeching noise from the secret door occurs. I'm surprised that I can't see the exit. I'm about to take a step forward, when an eerie voice says, "I'll give you a hint. You already know him."

"Who are you?" I demand, searching through the darkness. His voice is smooth and familiar.

153

I hear his footsteps coming closer, tapping against the concrete floor, "Don't come any closer!" I warn.

He continues his smooth strides, and then he comes into view, pointing a small handgun directly at my face, "Or what?"

I see his face, and gasp. Ordell, my driver. I feel my heartbeat speed up dramatically.

"Ordell." I say, firmly. Would he really kill me?

"Nobody has called me Odie in a long time."

I think about how the name relates. I guess that Ordell has both O and D. Odie.

"Not since my mother died, I bet." I say, being cautious to not aggravate him. What's the relation between them? How does my mother know Ordell?

He clicks a bullet into the chamber of the gun, "That would be correct."

I think back to the initials on the portrait and point to it, "You painted that picture, didn't you?"

He nods, "I did that one for free. Last painting, I ever did. After Kristene died, I stopped painting."

At first, I thought his words were sentimental. But they weren't.

Suddenly, three shots ring out of his gun. The noise combined with the anticipation of pain drains my body of motion. But they don't hit me. I glance behind me where there are now three holes in my mother's portrait. He has perfect aim—it hit her eyes and mouth.

I turn back to Ordell and purse my lips, "Why are you trying to kill me?"

"It's not just you," He responds, chuckling, "I need to kill your mother too."

"She's already dead."

"Not necessarily. Our group has a way of... living."

"Your group?"

He nods off the question, and changes the topic, "I used to be a general, back in the war. I worked next to your father. I was fired when the war ended, so I got a job in the government."

"And Atrox tasked you with killing me."

"Atrox tasked me with watching you," he snaps, "To gain your trust, so I could—"

"Disorient me." I say, cutting him off.

"Don't interrupt me," he warns, lifting the gun to my face. He licks his lips, "I've always had my own agenda. Atrox may want to keep you alive, but I need to kill you." He still hasn't answered my question. Why does he want to kill me?

"But why?" I regret interrupting.

He ignores my words anyways, and finishes his words, "I'm going to kill you, whether Atrox wants me to or not."

I realize now that he's stepped very close. He's only three feet away, and the gun is still pointed to

155

my face. I brace myself for the attack. What will it feel like?

Suddenly, a powerful force rips Ordell from his position. I don't see who at first, but they quickly pin him to the ground. Soldiers. They wear their navy-blue uniforms and it's almost impossible to see them in the darkness.

"I'm afraid that won't be necessary, Mr. Ordell," says a voice by the door, "And if it is ever necessary, then I'll do it myself."

I immediately recognize the voice. President Atrox. I can hear him walking closer.

The soldiers have Ordell on his stomach, and his arm is twisted behind his back. A gun is pointed to the back of his head, but I notice that the safety switch is on.

Atrox finally comes into view, looking paler in the darkness, "Thank you, sir." I stutter while saying this. I'm hoping that he doesn't see my mother's portrait behind me—although it's out in the open, so the thought is ridiculous.

"A thank you won't be necessary," he lifts his chin while glaring towards me, "What were you doing here?"

I sigh in relief, thankful that he doesn't know about my mother's letter. If he knew, then he'd probably kill me or Amica instantly, "Well, you sent me here, I think. Didn't you?"

"I did not intend for you to come here. I didn't even know this room existed," he glances behind me towards the portrait. I hold my breath, hoping he doesn't recognize her, "Who's that in the portrait?"

I finally release my breath, "I'm not sure. Ordell shot the eyes and mouth before I could recognize her."

Thank you, Ordell. Now that I look at it, he's made it unrecognizable. The thought sparks another thought. Did he shoot the painting so I wouldn't get in trouble with Atrox? It seems far-fetched considering he was going to kill me himself.

"Very well then. You may leave."

I nod and leave immediately. Questions are coursing through my mind. How did Atrox find me? What is up with Ordell? I definitely don't know the full story yet, and I realize that I might never know what's truly going on.

As I exit the building, I notice my limo sitting by the curb. I climb in quickly, and notice that the blonde driver has returned. I guess he's the new permanent driver since Ordell's as good as dead.

Goosebumps flood my arms as I think about this. It's disturbing how Atrox can kill so easily. Although it also comforts me since I now feel safer.

The driver begins driving, and I decide to not ask his name. After Ordell, it feels best to not establish a connection with my driver. Instead, I ask, "Excuse me, could you take me to Oraculi Sceptor's house?"

He nods his head.

I have no idea what prompted the thought, but for some reason, I find myself wanting to stand in his presence. He always knows what to say.

As the drive drags on, I think about how crazy this is. He probably won't even want to see me. How do I know he's even home from his new government job?

A tiny thought squeezes its way into my mind, and I remember the small interaction we had earlier. Was he mad at me? I asked his score, which could be disrespectful to a slave, but it shouldn't be a problem for a Magna member. I do understand how it could be sensitive, but his reaction seemed strange. It seemed like a reaction I would have. Or one like Amica would have.

The more I think about it, the more I realize the rebellious nature of his response. He said that the test doesn't define who we are. It's definitely true, but the quote seems out of place for Eli.

However, it's too late to turn back now. The driver is pulling into the driveway of a mansion. It's not a Beta house and it's a few miles from the Presidential circle. There's no official Magna mansion neighborhood, but they're all near each other. It surprises me that Eli is still in his mansion.

As I exit the car, I examine the exterior. He has no garage, so his sleek black car sits out in the open. Somehow, I get the feeling that he's just gotten home. I see him hanging his coat through the window. I watch as his eyes glance outside, and he jumps when he notices me.

Since I'm exposed now, I walk to the door. He's ahead of me, and is already opening the door while greeting me, "Hello, Ms. Kingston. I wasn't expecting you."

Neither was I, honestly. However, I'm here so I must respond, "Well, something bugged me a little bit. About what you said to me earlier."

"Well, come in." As he says this, I warm up. He's invited me in, so I don't think he's as mad as I thought. Relief courses through me, and I walk in slowly.

I stop walking in the foyer, and stop to talk to him here, "You said that the test doesn't define who we are. And that's true, but I've thought about it some more."

I hesitate to say the next part, and can't seem to find the words in my mind, "And?" He says, almost as though he's bored—although his tone isn't boredom. It's curiosity.

"And I'm just wondering... Are you against Pura?"

What happens next is unexpected. He grabs me by the arm and drags me into the house. I resist for a second, but I can tell that he's mad at something. But it's not me.

He drags me under the staircase, and I instantly know why he's brought me here. There aren't any security cameras.

"Alice, listen to me. Stay out of this. You need to be more careful. This is serious stuff, and there's a lot more going on than you know."

His words shock me, and I pull my arm from his grasp, "I can handle myself. And I do know what's going on," I pause, before continuing, "At least on my end."

"What do you mean on your end?" He asks, skeptically.

I've said too much. Now I have to tell him about my mother. So, I do. I tell him about Mutated Cerebrum, and Ordell, and how Atrox captured him. I even tell him about Amica, and that mess. Eli seems shocked at my words, and he's genuinely surprised that all this happened without him noticing.

"I will stay as safe as I can, but I still need to find out what's going on. My mother's letter didn't give me everything I needed to know."

I pull the medical records from my pocket. My hand almost grabs the letter, but I hesitate. The letter needs to stay with me.

"Here are the M.C. medical records. I need your help to find other people with the condition. Or just anything about it," As I hand them to him, I get nervous. These can't fall into the wrong hands. It feels like I can trust him. He's the smartest person in the city. I may appear to be but he seems to be so much more knowledgeable. Especially in this space, considering his medical and science experience from the Magna affiliate's program. Slowly, I begin to grasp why I came here. *Help*.

He takes the records quickly, and folds them neatly, before sliding them into his back pocket, "I'll run searches, and find whatever I can. But I don't want you to go too deep into this. It will only result in you getting yourself killed."

His arm pats my shoulder lightly, but I pull away quickly, "Eli, this is my family's business. I'll go as deep as I want."

He apologizes, and I know that he's truly sincere. He just wants to protect me. And I want to protect him. It's strange, but it feels as though we now have an unspoken agreement to protect each other.

Chapter 16

I RETURN TO my home shortly after. Without much effort, I fall asleep. My sleep is filled with dreams of Ordell being pinned to the ground. Gunshots ring in the background. Every time it happens, I get a rush. The same rush I felt when he pointed the gun at me.

As the night goes on, the dreams get longer, and more intense. In one, Atrox's soldiers pin Ordell to the floor, and then they all laughed. I wanted to attack them all, but I couldn't.

The last dream I have was the worst of them all. I once again watch Ordell being pinned to the ground, but this time somebody else emerges from the darkness. Eli. Only, something is different. He points a gun to my face as well. Another shot goes off, but Eli falls to the floor. I run to help him—seemingly forgetting that he's pointed a gun to my face—but Atrox now emerges from the darkness. Anger boils within me, and I rush to attack him. Right as I land a punch, I wake up.

I jolt awake, and my breathing has rapidly accelerated. I put my hand to my forehead and notice that my left temple is wet. I rub it for a second in hopes of getting rid of the splitting headache.

When I bring my hand back down, my fingers aren't covered in sweat. They're covered in blood. Red, thick blood. A single drop rolls off my finger and onto the blanket.

I clap my other hand over my mouth and bite my tongue, so I don't scream. This is not a dream.

I slip out from under the blanket—careful to not let the blood touch it—and rush to the bathroom. As I look in the mirror, I hardly recognize myself.

My left temple is covered in a huge scrape. Blood flows swiftly, pouring out from the center of the wound, and down my face.

I rush back into the bedroom and search my bed for large stains. No stains are there—other than the small droplet I just dropped—and it surprises me. A wound this big would have easily gotten blood on the pillow.

Only one thought comes to mind. *Somebody has been here.* They hurt me and cleaned up very well so

I wouldn't remember. I walk back to the bathroom, calmer than before. I clean the wound and dry it slowly. Once it's clean, the blood stops flowing, and it looks a bit better. You can still see the rugged surface that now occupies my forehead. It's going to leave a scar.

I think about Auxillio now. She'll be furious with me. My next speech is tomorrow. This gives me an even worse headache. She'll be here soon to plan. I do my best to cover the wound with spare makeup I find in the cabinets. I've never used any before, but I rub a substance that is the color of my pale skin over the wound. I wince as it touches the scrape but grit my teeth and push through.

The doorbell goes off downstairs, and a ringing sound bellows through the halls. I rush downstairs, and find Auxillio hanging her coat, and setting down her purse.

She takes one look at me and screams, "Alice! What happened to your forehead?"

Her face displays horror, and I'm disappointed by my efforts to cover it, "It's even worse than this. I did my best to cover it up."

She steps back, "What happened?"

I explain to her how I woke up, and don't remember it at all. We decide to ask a passing by slave, and he says, "We heard some shuffling and banging around in your room, but we didn't want to interrupt you."

I glare at him, "You guys can interrupt me all you want. I don't need slaves."

He smiles and thanks me. However, I insist on thanking him.

"All right, let's go to the study." I tell Auxillio.

We walk there quickly and get right to work. She helps me to format the speech, and we write it together. I feel as though we've finished too quickly, because we're done by the afternoon.

"Auxillio, is it possible that we went too fast?" I ask, hoping she says no.

"It's a possibility," she pauses, "Or perhaps we've gotten better."

I'd like to believe we did good because of Auxillio's enthusiasm. However, I still have a gut feeling that tells me we should keep going. I know that Amica's life is on the line, yet I don't feel a sense of motivation. Maybe it's because we wrote the speech perfectly. Or maybe it's because I'm preoccupied with the horrors of yesterday, and especially last night.

I send Auxillio home, "All right, I'll be back by one."

She moves along merrily, but I stop her quickly, "Auxillio, it's two. The next one is—"

"Tonight! I know." She replies, cutting me off.

"Why would you be here at one in the morning?" I ask, irritated. She explains that the speech tomorrow is at eight in the morning. I sigh and send her off.

After she leaves, I decide to go get lunch at a normal dining location. I'm tired of all the fancy Magna Council meals, and Beta mansion food. I need something good.

While I leave the house, I call Amica in hopes of us discussing the speech. I think about what we used to talk about. Friendship, war, studying, and complaining about student housing. It wasn't great topics to discuss, but I miss these conversations now more than ever. Now Amica's life is threatened thanks to me. I should have left her as a slave. It would have been easier for both of us. And much safer.

When I get into the limo, I ask the man to drive me to the park near the protesting lot. I'm not sure if I choose that area for the food stands, or for the protesters. The drive is quick but feels so slow.

I climb out of the car, and perch myself at the designated meeting location on a bench. I can see the protesting lot from here. I slip on sunglasses in a pitiful effort to hide my face. The protesters scream for a few minutes, and then stop to talk to each other. The pattern seems to repeat consistently.

They hold signs, and some even have guns clipped to their belts. Men, women, and even some teenagers occupy the lot. It makes me sick to know that so many of them died thanks to me. They attacked me because of my actions and were forced to pay the ultimate price.

My thoughts are cut off by a kind voice behind me, "Hey, Alice."

It's Amica—as I suspected. Her voice is slightly subdued, but I decide to ignore it. She asks why I called her here, "I wanted us to talk. About the speeches. I want your opinion, because I can't keep gambling with your life."

She chuckles while responding, "I'd trust you with my life ten times."

"Only ten?" I tease.

We both laugh. It's been so long since we've laughed together. It reminds me of what I used to be like. When the sun shined brighter, and I wasn't so cold from Atrox breathing down my neck.

We begin talking about the speeches. I read the new one that Auxillio and I wrote today. She pauses before saying she likes it. Her silver eyes avert to the side while speaking, and she brushes her hair out of her eye. I've known Amica for a while, and her hair is never in her face. She's lying.

"Amica, I need you to be honest," I say, glaring at her, "This is *your* life we're talking about."

Yet she still assures me that it's great. I nod. I can only hope that she's right.

Chapter 17

I STAND IN the Presidential Office, while my stomach churns. Auxillio and I tweaked the speech slightly, and we're minutes away from presenting.

Auxillio begins pulling me to the balcony, but President Atrox pulls me over, "Auxillio, give us a second."

She nods—irritated—and walks away, "What do you need." I ask, firmly.

"Alice, I don't need anything. Think about the people. If you fail, then you'll spark another war that kills humanity."

As the words soak into my brain, my breaths become raspy. They're fast paced, and not deep enough. His words echo within my mind. *You will kill humanity.* I vaguely remember him saying, if I fail, but I practically already know I'll fail. Don't I? Not only will I kill Amica, but everybody else too. How did I not see the power of my words? I find myself longing to be in student housing once again. Life was simpler back then, I ate, went to school, and had the occasional conversation with Tabitha.

I hear his words fading back into my mind, "Good luck."

Good luck, good luck, good luck. I'm going to need it. Did he just say that? I can't keep track of who's saying what. It's all blending together, and it reaches a crescendo before Auxillio finally yells, "No! You must go to the balcony, now!"

Her brow is sweating, and I can tell she's frustrated because Atrox made us late. *If you fail, then you kill humanity.*

As Auxillio pushes me onto the balcony, Atrox's words still linger throughout my mind. They narrow down until the true meaning is apparent, *you will kill humanity.*

A camera is only a few feet from my face, and it's difficult to focus my eyes. Everything feels blurry.

The blinking red light begins, and I know the broadcast has begun. As I reach the railing on the balcony, I can see the thousands of spectators. I hear reactions from the crowd, but it's too difficult to decipher. Their screams pierce through me, and out the other side.

169

I have trouble regaining my breath, but I need to focus, "Welcome Pura City, to another gathering regarding the future of humanity," That wasn't the correct opening line. My breaths get deeper, but not in a good way, "In the last speech, I spoke about our society, and it's perfection."

The only thought that floats in my mind is, *that's not the right line.* What is the right line? I can hear Auxillio groaning behind me. Now it's confirmed. Somehow, I've forgotten the speech. I do the only thing I can. Improvise.

"Like I said in the last speech, *anybody* should be willing to sacrifice themselves for humanity. In the last war, we simply stretched ourselves too thin. We now have no other option. We must pay the price."

The speech has completely disappeared from my mind, and I now say whatever I can think of, "If there were to ever be another war, then we would be encouraging the loss of human life."

Atrox's words still stay in my mind. I have to fight to not say them out loud, "If there were to ever be another war, then we would be encouraging the loss of human life." *Wait, I already said that.*

Everything seems strange now. As if the world has changed. Even my mental thoughts seem distant. Like they're not mine. It feels like I'm watching a blurry television, with a horrible narrator.

The Novus

It gets to the point where I can hardly hear or control what I'm saying. Am I even saying anything? Or am I just standing silently? It's all confusing, and I don't seem to have control.

It's too late. My speech is all messed up, and now Amica will die. Atrox has probably already sent soldiers to assassinate her. This thought helps me to focus, and I end the speech quickly. I need to save Amica.

"Now, our city is run beautifully, thanks to the Magna Council. Pura City will live on forever!"

The ending was horrible. The entire speech was much shorter than it was supposed to be. I spin around quickly, before the audience breaks out in ridicule. Shouts and screams erupt from the crowds, so I run in faster.

I glance around the office. Everybody's face is stricken in sorrow and they avoid my gaze. Even Eli's face displays a look—although his is more sympathetic. He's the only one who now knows what will happen.

Atrox stands in a corner talking to two soldiers. He exits the room through a side door, and the soldiers begin pacing towards me.

"Ms. Kingston, come with us." The woman on the left grabs my arm to pull, but I quickly pull away.

"I can walk myself." I snap.

She nods, and embarrassment crosses my face. Even I'm sorry for myself. But I'm sorrier for Amica. I need to get to her.

The soldiers lead me through the halls, and I wonder if I can slip out quickly. Even though I know I can't. The guards are bigger and faster than me. They'll stop me before I can complete two steps. They lead me down yet another hall, and we begin to go deeper into the Pura building. I get nervous as we go down—as though they'll throw me into a cell like they did with my mother.

We go down another few levels, and it's now obvious that we're underground. There are still windows, but they are artificial with nothing more than a screen behind them.

We pass by labs, and experiment rooms. One room we pass is an observatory. Behind the glass are all kinds of rare species. One strange snake-like creature hisses at me. I only get a short glance, but they're truly exotic animals.

They push me past the observatory and bring me to an adjacent room. They shove me inside and lock the door behind me. I'm left inside, alone.

I glance around the unfamiliar room. Tapestries hang along the faces of each wall. The back wall has an emergency exit door, and I debate going through—I rule it out, because an alarm would probably go off.

Since I have nothing else to do, I focus on the hanging tapestries. Upon inspection, I notice that they each represent a battle or war. They each have a date in the bottom right corner. Some date back thousands of years.

Each one is intricately woven. They hang in order, and I walk around the entire room before I come upon the last war. It shows the Atrox brothers standing, backs turned to each other. There is a one-foot gap, and then it shows thousands of soldiers fighting one another. They are only tiny dots, yet you can easily tell what they are. Within the gap are bombs circling around the Atrox brothers.

It displays the war. The Atrox brothers stand in the center, commanding the bombs to explode the helpless soldiers. Everything outside the image is a deep black, which represents the rest of the world in ashes.

As I gaze upon the ugly tapestry—now focusing on each individual loop—the familiar tapping of dress shoes comes closer. My flesh tightens as I try to find a hiding spot.

I run to the back of the room but realize that he sent me here for a reason. There's no way out. He wouldn't provide an exit for me—except the emergency exit, but they would catch me easily.

The door creaks open slowly, and President Atrox walks in. My pulse accelerates at the sight of him. He searches the room with his eyes, before locking them on mine.

"How dare you."

His words aren't what I imagined they would be. What did I dare to do? Then, I realize seconds later. I dared to practically destroy his city and spark another war. I struggle to form words, but they pour out soon after, "What you told me before the show, it made me nervous. I couldn't remember the real speech." I stutter on every word, and he probably can't even hear me over my sobs.

"Pitiful," His expression deepens, and he looks more despicable than normal. He walks closer as he goes on, "I would bet that this speech was worse than the first. Anybody watching could hear the quiver in your voice. Anybody could see that you were saying words but didn't believe them yourself!"

He screams for me to stand up. I didn't even realize that I was on the floor crying.

"This is the hall of wars Ms. Kingston. Every documented war holds a place here. There will be another one thanks to you."

The fact slaps me in the face. It is my fault. There will be another war, and it's all my fault. How did I gain this position? I struggle to remember anything at this point.

"Alice, I've plotted to kill you many times. I've kept you alive for many reasons, but the biggest reason is to get what I need out of you. Killing you would be showing mercy," he grins, "So instead, I provide an alternative. I'll be following through with our deal."

I know what that means, "No. Please no, take me instead!" I'm pleading, and begging I fall to the floor beneath him. His words ring in my mind, *but the biggest reason is to get what I need out of you.* I didn't know what he meant at first, but now I do. He wants to take everything away from me. This is his final action to destroy my Mutated Cerebrum.

"Your friend will die today. A team of combatant soldiers are already assassinating her right now."

I immediately stop crying. The sorrow and sobs turn into fear, which morphs into anger. If he won't kill me, then I can still hurt him. I raise my hand and swing it across his face with every ounce of strength I contain. As my hand goes back down, I can already see a red spot where the bruise will be.

I do my best to reciprocate his evil grin. I will not let him see me weak.

He tries to retort with a smirk, but the effects of my slap have depleted his confidence for a split second. With that, I run to the emergency exit and push through the door. As I suspected, an alarm goes off, and I grin at the thought of causing havoc in the Pura building. Inside the exit is a very long staircase.

I glance behind me, and I freeze as I see how deep the staircase goes. *I'm exposed.* But I grit my teeth and run up the stairs. I must trip at least two times but keep going. When I finally reach the top, I push through the exit.

I come out into a garden supplies area. All I can think about is where I would find Amica. It's my only hope. She wouldn't just be standing in her home, not today. There's no way they've already found her either.

I purse my lips as I trip yet again. It's the dress. My dress is stopping me, so I pull it up and tie it into a loose knot. It's not pretty, but it works. I also take off my shoes and rip off the heels. Then, I continue running.

I'm much faster now and have made up for lost time. Now, where would Amica be? I debate whether she was watching the speech. Surely, she was smart enough to go somewhere unpredictable in case if she would be assassinated. She would obviously watch it later. So, where else could she be? Since she's not at her house, she might be running errands for her mother.

Looking ahead, I notice that the light is red, but will turn green any second. The crosswalk will close, and I can't afford to lose that time. The crosswalk is probably sixty feet away. *I can make it.* All I need is hope.

The red stoplight begins to fade as if it's in slow motion. Some cars are already beginning to inch forward, and I begin to doubt my speed. I have to make it. I'm less than twelve feet away when the light completely turns green. Cars are already moving, and have filled the roads in seconds, however, I'm already moving as well, and can't seem to stop. I still move forward. I commit to running through and do my best to avoid cars. Horns honk, and people scream through their windows, but I don't care. I need to run.

Then, I notice a large truck coming down the street. This is one of the busiest roads, yet somehow, I still believe I can make it. My feet weave between the cars, and the large truck meets the road one second behind me. I run forward as quickly as possible, and I can't stop now. I have to go. My feet propel me forward, and I make it past less than a second before I feel the leftover wind from the truck. It almost grazes my back, and I don't dare breathe yet. Just a little further. I accelerate once again, and arrive at the other side, with nothing but sore legs.

I run past the city circle, wasting no time. I've settled on the idea that Amica is running errands. She doesn't have a lot of money, so she's probably at the cheapest store. The student store.

It's probably six blocks from here. It feels too far, it should take maybe six minutes. Six minutes seems too long, and it's thanks to the busy sidewalks. I get the idea to call for my limo, so I go into my Magna contacts. While scrolling through, I notice that they've been disabled. I squeeze my fist in frustration.

There's no escape from running. I have to run all the way. The streets are less crowded than I expected. Especially as I go farther out into the city. After around four minutes, I arrive at the string of stores that occupy the area. As I rush through, I find the student store instantly.

Somebody pushes open the door, and I take the opportunity to get through. I run to the first aisle, and it's completely empty. In fact, the store is almost completely deserted. Only a few families walking around. Then, I glance towards the door, and see a familiar face walking towards it.

"Amica!" She doesn't hear me, but I look past her and through the store window where soldiers are running down the street, filtering through the crowds. I scream her name again, and I can see her slowly shift.

She searches the store with her eyes, and they finally set on mine. I'm relieved, but the soldiers will be inside any second.

I run to Amica and grab her arm before she can react. I lead her to the back of the store. As we duck behind an aisle, the lights go out, and the gunshots begin.

Chapter 18

BULLETS CASCADE ACROSS the store. Soldiers are shouting orders to each other repeatedly, "Cover aisle two!"

"Get eyes on the target!"

Those words send a shiver down my spine, and I notice a soldier running along the back of the store. Towards us. They're not shooting yet, because they're waiting for a clear shot. Then, I realize that they see me. They can't kill me, so, I place my body in front of Amica's.

The soldier slows down as he realizes who I am, "Ms. Kingston, you have to move immediately. That's an order!"

"I'm above you. Clear out! That's an order." I yell this out, hoping they'll listen. But I know they won't. I'm simply buying time.

The soldier finally reaches Amica and I, and attempts to shove me out of the way with his hand. Instead, I latch onto it, and kick his leg in the process. I kick hard and he falls, lying flat on his stomach.

Amica reaches down swiftly and grabs his gun. I don't think she knows how to shoot, so I'm not sure what she thinks she'll do with it.

A bullet whizzes past my head—too close to be at Amica. They're aiming at me now as well. I grab Amica's hand and drag her to the next aisle.

Screams bellow through the store, but the soldiers don't care. I hear people drop to the floor with a thump. Tears glide down Amica's face, but we can't stop now. We have to get out. They won't stop until they find her. A gunshot goes off as we run to the next aisle.

Suddenly, the entire store falls silent. I don't think everybody's dead—yet—but instead the remaining people are hiding. I can't believe that even Atrox would allow this. He's killing innocent civilians.

I hear footsteps approaching near us, and Amica and I huddle closer together—hoping to conceal ourselves in the darkness. I hold my breath—ready to attack—and feel Amica's hand grip the gun tighter. Finally, the soldier walks directly in front of us. Only, it's not a soldier. It's a broad-shouldered man, who's at least six feet tall. He wears a fine suit, and sunglasses. His long brown hair is smoothed into a slick mass at the back of his head. Eli. I allow myself to breath as he crouches down.

I feel Amica tensing up, and I realize that she doesn't know who he is. So, I whisper into her ear, "It's Oraculi Sceptor. You can trust him."

The word *trust* quiets her, and she relaxes. A soldier's footsteps echo off the tiled flooring, and I estimate how close they are. Probably ten to fifteen feet away. I try to imagine what he looks like by sound. The ball of his foot hits at a slower pace, so it's probably a man with big feet. I can hear a subtle break in the pattern of his breathing. He doesn't want to do this.

He's less than five feet away from us, but there's nothing we can do now. If we move, then we give up our location.

I peak my head out through a small hole concealed by a kitchen supplies stand. I now realize how Atrox can do this. He's disguised them in outer Colony uniforms. They have a strange seal on their coats. I don't recognize the specific seal, but it has a tiny dot in the corner that indicates that they're not from Pura City. Since I don't recognize the specific seal, it's impossible to identify their actual colony. The only one I've heard of is Rahjo.

I've never seen it, or been there, but it's the closest colony to Pura City.

As I examine the soldier's uniform more, I begin to wonder if all colony invasions have been organized by President Atrox. It's a great method for him to kill, without creating suspicion against himself.

I try not to think about it, because now the soldier is less than three feet away. The almost silent noise from his boots stabs my ears. Like a countdown to death. When he's less than two steps away, I decide I have no other choice. In less than a second, I've spun around—out of Eli's grasp—and delivered a hit to the soldier's stomach.

The hit wasn't harmful, but it took him by surprise. I wrestle him for his gun, while shouting for Amica to run. She doesn't move, but instead comes over to help me. Eli joins in as well. It makes me angry that they didn't listen, but it only fuels me more. I easily pry the gun from the soldier's grip, but I soon realize that he simply let go.

He ducks behind the aisle in an attempt to hide, and whispers to me, "Please don't shoot, I have kids."

I don't respond to him and decide that we need to move. We leave him there, and sprint towards the back of the store. I hold the gun up while running—only as a threat. As we reach the back corner, guns ricochet bullets near the front of the store. They've found some hiding people.

Amica runs before I can stop her, "Stop Amica! We have to go!"

But she doesn't stop. In fact, she pretends to not hear me. Amica has a mind for helping people, which is the opposite of myself.

I have to at least help Amica. So, I swallow my feelings, and chase her.

By the time I catch her, she's helping people escape the store. A little girl—probably eight years old—runs towards Amica but slides on shattered glass. She falls to the floor, and I watch her arm snap.

All logic has escaped my body, and I run to her aid, through the gunfire.

She lies on the floor, and a bullet lands near her head. I can't possibly imagine that they'd aim at her. I scoop her up quickly, but not before a bullet grazes my arm. I wince, and my arm goes limp—dropping the girl. It's excruciating, and I can't possibly imagine what a real shot would feel like. Blood is already leaking out of the wound.

"Alice Kingston, you are interfering with a—"

He's cut off when he falls to the floor unconscious. Eli stands behind him holding a crowbar. In fact, I notice that the rest of the soldiers lay in similar positions. Amica is standing over one as well. I smile and attempt to scoop the girl back up. She's fallen unconscious now as well.

"We have to go now!" orders Amica.

As she says this, I drop the girl once again, and tell them about my arm wound. Eli inspects it for a second, and then lifts the girl himself. I notice a similar wound on his arm, yet he grits his teeth and carries on.

We all run quickly. The soldiers will wake up soon, but they won't shoot since we're gone. Everybody else will be safe and escorted to a hospital. Except for the ones who didn't make it.

Amica, Eli, and I, all run to the alley behind the store. I stop them and say, "Amica, before we go any further, you need to leave the city now."

"Why?" She asks, and I realize she doesn't know why the soldiers were there.

"Those weren't real colony soldiers. They were Pura soldiers in disguise to kill you," I pause, still feeling the pain in my arm, "The deal with Atrox is off. He's trying to kill you."

She nods and asks where she's supposed to go. I'm at a loss for words, but Eli chimes in, "You can sneak out of Pura. Try to find one of the colonies."

It's not a great suggestion, but it's the only option. There's no way she could hide here and survive. They'd find her.

"I don't know where they are!"

Eli stops to think once more, but finally answers, "If you go east, you'll find either Rahjo, or Praelia."

The Novus

I nod in agreement. I've never heard of Praelia, but I'll take his word for it. Amica glares at me as though she wants to say goodbye, but instead turns away and runs. It's horrible that she can't give me a proper goodbye but this is the way it has to be.

I hardly have any time to think about what's happened, because the little girl in Eli's arms squirms uncomfortably. She tells him that she thinks her arm is broken. He nods, and we run to the hospital.

We leave the girl at the hospital but couldn't contact her mother. She's dead.

Eli and I return to the alley where Amica left, and we crouch down low. It doesn't feel safe to go back into the public.

It's embarrassing, but I begin to cry. I cry right in front of Eli, massive sobbing, that echoes off the alley walls. He sits next to me and wraps his arm around my shoulders. It doesn't feel loving, but instead feels kind. I can't decide which one I'd rather have.

I ignore Eli's arm and begin mourning over Amica's inevitable death. Nobody ever survives after they leave the city. The government restricts us from having too much knowledge about the colonies, so nobody really knows who or where they are.

Amica will travel for miles—probably in the wrong direction—and then die a slow painful death from dehydration or hunger.

My thoughts shift, and I realize that I haven't changed anything in the city. I should have been using my power for good. Instead, I've written out Amica's death sentence. The thought encourages more tears to explode.

I should begin writing my death sentence as well. Atrox will no doubt try to find Amica. He'll go to any length. The only thing that protects me is the public eye. If I die, then the citizens will only get angrier.

Eli removes his arm from my shoulder—somehow sensing that I want to stand up. When I do, he follows me to my feet. A thought hits me. It feels too early to think like this, but Amica wouldn't want me to waste any time. It reminds me of how I rushed into the deal with Atrox. Logically, I should wait. But my logic has failed me up to this point.

If Amica's gone for good, then I have nobody to protect but myself. I'm free. I can do what I set out to do in the beginning. What Amica would have wanted. I'm going to use my power to protest.

I'm going to use my power to save Pura City.

As I collect my thoughts, we get ready to leave, "Alice, before we go, I need to give you something," he pauses, while pulling papers out of his pocket, "It's all I could scrape up on Mutated Cerebrum."

I receive the papers, and respond, "That was quick."

"It's why I found you in the store. I wish I took more time to research, but I didn't know what would happen to you after the speech."

While he speaks, I begin to thumb through the papers. It's only three sheets. One is a medical record, one is a picture, and the last is an article.

I begin with the article. My eyes scan over it quickly, and I find that it talks about the specifics of M.C. While it makes you smarter in many ways, there's one weakness. M.C. is a very fragile condition. You can easily lose it. Anything that disorients you can bring you back to a standard brain level. That's why President Atrox agreed to not kill me. He knew that he could break me easily.

So, this is why I've felt less smart recently. All these events are making me weaker. It's not a total loss though, because now I have leverage. I know what's wrong, and I can fix it. I just need to stay strong, and ahead of Atrox.

The next paper is a picture of a toddler. It's a small slip of paper, but the child looks familiar. It's a young boy, and I assume that he must be the only other person with the condition. But who is it? I assume that I'll find out in the medical record.

I begin at the top of the paper. Written in clear letters is the name I'd least suspected. *Oraculi*

Sceptor. Eli has Mutated Cerebrum. I glance at him for a brief second, slightly angry that he didn't say anything. I look at the date and do the math in my head. They documented his case when he was fourteen years old, which was after mine.

As I continue reading, everything begins to feel darker. When I'm finished, I begin to question him, "Why didn't you tell me?"

He hesitates before answering, "I didn't know, just like you. I found out this morning. We're the only documented cases in *history*."

The thought seems odd. It's a huge coincidence that we both have M.C. and have managed to meet each other. Out of the many people that have lived, *we* met. Although I know why. President Atrox.

The dots connect in my mind quickly. Something greater than us has pulled us together. And I fear that the same thing will pull us apart.

Chapter 19

TODAY'S EVENTS LEAVE me discouraged, yet a small part of me recognizes a victory. My conversation with Eli might have left us avoiding each other, but I'm free from Atrox.

He holds no power over me now.

I don't feel great about how Amica's situation concluded, but it leaves me free of stress. I know what I must do now. I have to honor Amica.

It's seven in the morning, and I've already called Zane, Nita, and Avetay. I left out Conso and Zed, because I have a feeling that they are loyal to Pura City.

We will be meeting in the park next to the protesting lot and preparing for the most important speech of my life. Even though Eli and

I are avoiding each other, I've invited him. He'll stand off to the side, and we won't talk.

This speech will be much more important than the others. I called Auxillio to tell her that I was letting her go—to keep her safe from all this—but she insisted that she would be fine. I didn't argue with that.

I exit the mansion and realize that I might never return. I frown. It was a very nice house. I walk down the long staircase and climb into Auxillio's car. She waits by the curb, humming a beautiful melody while waiting patiently.

None of us will arrive in our limos, but instead, we've arranged rides. Auxillio drives me there quickly and silently. When we reach the protesting lot, I direct her to the adjacent park.

I thank her, and request for her to stay nearby. Just in case. Before I exit the car, I slip on sunglasses to hide my face until we're ready.

When I exit the car, I immediately see them all sitting at a picnic table. They wave me over. As I walk, I wonder how we'll manage to change things with only four people. I brush the thought from my mind. No negativity. Not now.

I join them at their table.

"So, I'm glad you've realized what you did was wrong, but why did you do the speeches in the first place?" asks Zane.

I explain *everything*. How Amica scored low on the test, how I bartered with the president, and how I failed so he tried to kill her. I say that I have no idea where she is now and can only hope that she'll make it to one of the colonies.

While I talk, they all nod their heads apologetically, "So what's the plan then?" Asks Avetay.

"We protest. The law says we can." I respond.

"But the law doesn't say that we can blow off Magna Council. We're required to go." Replies Avetay.

Finally, I end the discussion, "It's debatable. The city allows us to protest and do strikes, so technically we're fine. The law also doesn't say anything about the Magna Council protesting, so we have loopholes."

They all agree. It makes sense. We could stand a chance in court. Not that we'd get to go to court. Atrox would make sure that we become slaves, or even captives. I'm not sure which is worse.

We begin to organize things. I send Auxillio and her assistants to make signs for us, while the rest of us work on what we'll say. The most important thing is for us to give inside information. We need to tell the citizens what's really happening inside Pura City. We are going to expose the president and his peers.

All of us will take part in the speech. The thing that makes it even better, is that we know the city's secrets. We've been here working inside the Pura building against our will. We have no choice, and neither do the thousands of slaves.

Zane has been quiet for a few minutes, but I don't notice until he speaks, "We shouldn't associate ourselves with the Magna Council anymore."

As he says this, I realize that it's true. For great publicity, we can't be called the Magna. People still won't like us, "What do you mean?"

"We should rename our group. We're not the Magna Council anymore, we've left them behind. Conso, and Zed are the remaining Magna members. I don't want any part in that anymore."

So, we all stop to think about what we should rename ourselves, "How did they name us in the first place?" questions Nita.

I remember. I'd read about it in a textbook called *The Origins of Pura*, "They translated the word *great* into an ancient language."

"Well, I think we can all agree that the word *great* doesn't describe the Magna at all."

We all sit there for the next few minutes while we try to create a name. At first, we try to come up with something off the top of our heads, but now we're translating. It seems silly to stress over this small detail, but the name needs to have meaning. Avetay finds a phone application that documents old languages and has the ability to translate. It is very limited; however, we select the same language they used for the Magna Council.

The Novus

Now, all we have to do is find words to translate. We go through a lot including, *powerful, wonderful,* and even *awesome* for some reason. We couldn't find any good ones, and these hardly described our vision.

After a few minutes, Avetay finally comes up with a good one, "What about *new?*"

We think. *New.* It has a nice ring to it, and it definitely describes our new group. We're new, and different from the Magna Council. We don't have the same wants, or goals. We want to change things, and what's a better word than *new?* It's a great word, but it comes down to translation.

"What does it translate to?" I ask.

Avetay pulls out her phone and types the word into the translator. As she presses the translate button, a smile crosses her face.

"What is it?"

"Novus."

It's perfect. We don't even have to discuss. The Novus is our new name. It sounds great and has meaning behind it. This name will resonate with the protesters in so many ways.

With that out of the way, Avetay asks, "What do we do when Atrox tries to attack us?"

"We use the law, and the public eyes to protect ourselves," I respond, "But there's still the opportunity for us to be arrested. So, step out now if you want."

"None of us are leaving," begins Nita, "We've seen what they do. Now, it's our turn."

The time comes for us to march into the protesting lot hand in hand. All four of us hold our signs. We walk through the opening in the fence, and onto the grass. Each blade of grass has been flattened onto the ground by the hundreds of protesters standing here.

As we walk in, we begin the planned chant. People around us seem confused. They look at us with hostile faces, wondering what we're doing here. Around fifteen seconds in, they realize that we're helping them.

We continue to chant, and people eventually join in. We march up into the front of crowd, where the space is cleared. In the center is a makeshift podium that the protesters have been using.

The other Novus members guide me forward and position me behind the podium. I will be speaking first. When I'm set, the chanting stops abruptly.

A silence follows as I look to my left and see Eli standing there quietly. It feels nice for him to be here, until I notice the look on his face. A look of despair. Something has happened.

I ignore it, because I have to continue. I take a deep breath, and introduce us, "Hello, as you all know, I'm Alice Kingston. *Former,* Magna Council member. I stand here today with a few other former members as well," I gesture behind myself, pointing to all of them, "We are here to stop the horrific acts being performed by our government. The government that enslaves innocent people."

I continue introducing the Novus. I explain how long we've felt this way, how we felt too scared to do anything about it, and the story about Amica. It feels great to tell everybody this story. It's full of twists, and I see people relating to it. So many others had loved ones become slaves. If I connect with them in any way, let it be that. Even though the story is depressing, I realize that I've had it better than most. At least I had the power and opportunity to fix my issue. It makes me think of things on a wider scale, and it's this thought that fuels my speech.

More reporters pull into the protesting lot, and I smile. Publicity is the key factor in getting what we want.

"I think we all remember a world where you were innocent until proven guilty," says Zane, "We've fallen into a barbaric pattern, governed by the true evil of our world."

Zane continues for a few minutes, and then steps down from the podium so Nita can talk, "As Zane said, we all used to be innocent until proven guilty. Right now, thousands of slaves are scattered around the city. Each one is innocent."

Finally, Avetay talks. Her story relates to me more than I expected, "I had a sister. Her name was Joelle, and she scored low on the test just like Amica did," she pauses, and I can tell that she's trying to stay strong. Her eyes begin gleaming with tears, "Unfortunately, I couldn't support the deal we made, and he killed her," she breathes in deeply, and I know she won't share anymore— although I'd like to hear the rest of the story, "Anyways, that isn't the kind of world I want to live in. Thank you."

As she finishes talking, I wonder what would have happened if the roles were reversed between us. Amica would be dead.

With that, I conclude, "The last thing I want to talk about today, is our president. I've feared him for so long, but now I'm free. I will no longer hide in his shadow." My eyes begin to fill with tears, but I wipe them away, "Like I said, Atrox was watching me. He threatened me and killed my mother." Gasps explode from the crowd. I can't bring myself to finish that story, "President Atrox will destroy everything if we give him the chance. We will stop him and make him pay for what he's done."

Screams erupt from the crowd, but in my mind it's silent. I did what I wanted to do. I spoke my mind. But a realization is planted in the back of my mind. It lingers there quietly, whispering. *This won't bring them back.*

The Novus

It's true. I can't deny it. Speaking about it won't bring them back. They're gone, and it's my fault. Zane's voice pierces its way into my mind, asking if he can speak. I step down without saying anything,

"We are leaving the Magna Council behind. This group is not a part of that anymore," he licks his lips before finishing, "In honor of that, we will be renaming the Magna Council, to the Novus. It means *new* in an ancient language, and that's what we're all about. Building a new city, and a new world. A better world, for everybody."

We finished our speech eight hours ago. Atrox has not yet said anything about the Novus not showing up for Magna duties. It worries me. I thought we would have been arrested by now. He hasn't made any public appearance at all.

After the speech, the Novus was interviewed by a lot of reporters. Most of them were directed towards me, but Avetay's story stuck with a lot of people. Especially me. I had no idea this was happening to her.

As the sky grows darker, many protesters go home. The Novus will be staying, along with the other hardcore protesters. A man delivers backpacks to the protesters who decide to stay.

While he pulls out a backpack for me, he says, "Crazy stuff going on these days," I nod, "Glad we got people like you to stick up for people like us."

He hands me the pack and moves on. The words were passive for him, but they remain in my mind. *Glad we got people like you to stick up for people like us.* His words had a larger impact than he intended, but the quote expands in my mind. Without them, I wouldn't be who I am today. I would be Alice Kingston, sitting in the Magna Council room, too afraid to do anything about it.

So, as I sit here in the freezing cold, I lie against the fence. His words echo within my head, as I fall down into the dark void that is my mind.

Chapter 20

ATROX HAS BEEN quiet. He's said nothing, and it's been a full two weeks since we started protesting. Perhaps he's organizing a way to kill us secretly, or to spin our protesting around for his benefit. Or the more likely option, he's preparing to negotiate with us.

The thought is empowering; Atrox needing to negotiate with us. But the fact that he's waited this long makes me nervous. He's doing something that I wouldn't expect. Preparing.

Besides worrying about him every day, these two weeks have been incredibly simple. I'd go as far as saying fun. For once in my life, I'm not on the Magna Council, or in a war, or even studying for the test. I'm fighting for people's rights, and it feels like my calling. It's not exactly sitting at home in a mansion, watching television, but it's soothing. My anger thrives, and I finally have a place to let it all out.

Every day has been the same. We wake up, and protest. Throughout the day, we run through chants, make speeches, and even occasionally scream as loud as possible.

The man who brought us backpacks on the first night brings us food, water, and extra blankets. I've never felt more alive.

It all seems too easy. I've even noticed less soldiers guarding us. All this leads me to one conclusion: Atrox is planning something. He must be preparing something. He's *lessened* his defenses since the Novus got here.

Perhaps he's putting together an elite military team to assassinate us. Or maybe he's decided to leave us alone, but never let us change anything. I know that the latter isn't true, yet I still hope that it is. A small part of my mind hopes that he's not planning something brutal. But he is.

It's about midday, and the protesters are quiet. We've stopped to talk, and I predict that speeches will follow after.

Minutes pass, and I decide to talk to Nita. She stands near a corner of the fence, and I greet her. She returns my greetings, and I ask, "What do you think we're doing next?"

She hesitates before responding, "Something's different. Somebody got word that a group of limos and military trucks are driving over."

I can physically feel my face drain of all color. Even Nita looks frightened by the sudden change in my face. I was right. Atrox is driving over in a limo, and the trucks are his protection.

Only one question stands out. What will he do? The military vehicles are either defense, or attack, so that's not very helpful information. Since Atrox is driving over, I'm willing to bet that he will be speaking to us. He's ready to negotiate. That, or drag us to the Pura building. But, he wouldn't drive all the way out for that.

The protesters are still silent, and I get the feeling that everybody's heard about the military escort. I begin hearing a loud buzz, that grows louder by the second.

Soon enough, the military trucks come into view. A temporary detour was set up, and the escort takes over all four lanes. They block the entrance of the fence, and I know that they're trapping us in. Perhaps they'll arrest everybody.

Doors of vehicles open, and close with a loud thump. People in all kinds of uniforms exit the cars—blue and gold military uniforms, specialty officers, and even suited agents. I can't see Atrox yet, but I'm absolutely certain that he's there. He's very short, so I assume that he's hidden by the wall of soldiers.

They march through the small gap they closed in the fence, and the crowd of protesters splits in two. There must be fifty soldiers walking up—probably more.

They march through the split of protesters, and a few soldiers run ahead to rip out the makeshift podium. They replace it with a smooth hardwood podium, lined with gold. A small detail, but a striking one. A simple act that screams, *we're more powerful than you.*

The group of soldier's crowd around the podium, and in less than a second, their guns are drawn. I wince—afraid that they'll shoot but realize that it's just to threaten us. I can feel everybody stiffen.

Finally, the group of soldiers splits open, and reveals President Atrox. He's shorter than I remember, but he wears a complex outfit. It's a velvet blue suit, with a golden tie. I realize that I've never seen him in such a public place, surrounded by so many people that despise him.

He starts talking earlier than expected, "Hello, citizens. I've come to inform you all of the law change. We're aware of the loop hole the Magna Council found in our law, so we changed it. Nobody—Magna or citizen—may refrain or go on strike from their job," he locks his eyes onto mine, "Effective immediately. Magna Council members have one hour to return to the Pura building. Punishments will be severe."

That's it. He hands his speech cards to an adjacent officer, and they walk away—guns still pointed directly at us.

His words hardly set into my mind by the time they drive away. *One hour.*

I know that he said one hour, but it doesn't feel real. Perhaps it's because he didn't identify what the punishment will be. It can't be anything. At least not for the Novus. He can't kill us—there'd be huge riots—and if he detained us in any way, then he'd still have riots. He has to know that— unless if this is what he's been planning for. He must have been preparing a strategy to defend against the riots for the past two weeks. If that's the case, then we've wasted our time. While we were screaming, he was planning. We should have paid attention to every detail. If we had, then we would have been prepared.

So, it's settled then. There's nothing we can do about it. If we don't go back to the Pura building, he'll punish us. Or worse—maybe he'll punish the rest of the protesters.

The military vehicles have gone out of sight, and somebody in the lot finally yells, "They can't punish the Novus. They must know that. They'd have violent protesting on their hands."

Everybody murmurs, and nods in agreement. Somebody else says "Well it's not just like we're going to give them up. They're our only chance."

Everybody agrees once again. But I don't. It seems like I'm the only one who knows what will happen. If we don't return, then all of them will probably die, or be made into slaves.

"No," I yell, firmly, "If the Novus doesn't return, then you all will either be killed, or made into slaves."

"Then we'll all go." I'm not sure who said it, but the idea makes sense. I don't like it at all, but I feel like I can't argue with them. I'm not sure why, until I realize that they've already begun running from the lot.

I sigh, knowing there's nothing I can do. I guess this plan is better than nothing.

The protesters begin yelling chants, but most just scream. They're drawing attention to themselves, and we're already wreaking havoc.

Cars swerve to the side as we sprint through the center of the road. It's not our goal to cause trouble, but it's the byproduct of protesting. I try to guess how long it will take us to reach the Pura building, but don't bother. We'll get there when we get there. Although I secretly hope that we don't get there at all. It will only result in the protesters being hurt, and the Novus being arrested.

I know that we've reached the Pura building when the crowd slows down. The government has put up a new fence and soldiers line the other side.

The Novus

While the crowd slows down, the screams get louder. A path splits the crowd in half for the Novus. We huddle together and walk up the gap slowly.

I step closer to the fence. It's a tall black fence, with vertical bars. I wonder if it's electrically charged.

The Pura building sits underneath a collection of clouds—which makes it look like an evil fortress. When we reach the fence, a gap between the soldier's forms. In the middle, a tall eight-foot man begins to pace towards us. He wears a specialty officer uniform—a navy blue uniform, lined with gold, along with a golden pauldron on his left shoulder. His chin is up, and his mouth is sealed. He wears sleek sunglasses, that create shadows under his eyes, and you can't see his forehead due to his military cap. Since he's taller, he reaches the fence in half the time it took us.

"Magna Council, you have no authority to quit your job," his voice is deep, and loud, "We hope you've decided to join us back in the Pura building."

He salutes as he finishes talking—which indicates that he still needs to respect us—which means that we have a little extra room to work, "Sir, we will not be joining you in the Pura building. We're tired of the cruel and unfair working conditions, along with the unnecessary slavery system."

I gulp when I finish talking.

"Magna Council workers are not in unfair working conditions."

"So being forced to sit in a dark room to make decisions for the city's government isn't unfair? We weren't given a choice. Not to mention the thousands of people who are enslaved." Argues Avetay.

The soldier's face seems to get darker as he says, "You have fifteen seconds before we arrest you."

He begins to count.

Chapter 21

Fifteen... fourteen... thirteen.

HE COUNTS IN a rapid pace. The protesters scream through the fence, directly to his face, "We want freedom!"

Ten... nine.

"You can try to arrest us all you want, but we have rights as citizens of the city!" yells Zane.

Eight... seven... six... five.

The crowd's screams are ear piercing at this point, "We have rights!"

Four... three...

He's not backing down. There's no way out now. I can't bring myself to scream.

Two...

"Stop!" yells a voice from behind the soldier. All the soldiers turn to the voice, and salute. President Atrox. The crowd falls silent in his presence. Nobody seems to have enough courage to scream in his face.

He's at least three feet shorter than the soldier and walks forward at a very slow pace. We end up standing silently for a minute.

He pulls over the soldier, "Commander Clint, this isn't your jurisdiction."

"I'm simply following orders, president. General Dune sent us."

"Well, General Dune didn't clear that with me." Replies Atrox.

They get into an argument over jurisdiction, but as usual, Atrox wins. He orders soldiers to take the tall man away.

"So, Magna Counc—"

"We're the Novus," I say, cutting him off, "We're not associated with the Magna Council anymore."

"Quitting isn't an option Ms. Kingston, and I think you know that."

It starts to become clear, that we don't stand a chance. I want to cower in a corner or run, but I know there's no way out.

Without thinking, I say, "We would rather be arrested, than to go back to work on the Magna Council."

The Novus

I regret it the second I say it. How could I volunteer us to be arrested? I should have asked them first. I think about seeing people arrested on television. They become slaves; I wonder what would happen to us. Atrox will likely throw us into a dungeon cell deep under the Pura building, and it's my fault. The Novus members will never forgive me.

I look back to Atrox, focusing my eyes on his cold stare. I can't let him win, "Fine. Have it your way," he says. He turns around as if we've disappeared, and yells to his soldiers, "Arrest them!"

The crowd behind us turns and runs, trying to get out before they're arrested too. I would like to do the same thing.

Instead, the Novus stands confidently in front of the soldiers. They're unlocking the fence in front of us. I catch a glimpse of Atrox walking away in the distance, and for some reason, I think about Tabitha watching me right now. I suppose it's because it all feels so distant. As if I'm viewing myself from a different perspective.

Finally, the soldiers push through the gate, and grab us. Two soldiers to one person. The soldiers that grab me are two large men. They look like what criminals used to be. Very big, with broad shoulders.

They begin dragging us away and I feel a faint prick. Soon enough, the world turns gray, and slowly fades into a deep black.

My eyes open, and the world has regained color. I lay propped up against a wall in a cell. The floor is white sand, and the walls are pure white. The bars to the cell are white as well and are formed into a grid pattern. I notice the Novus members leaning against it, staring at me.

I swallow, but find my mouth dry, "I'm sorry." My voice comes out in a hoarse whisper.

"Look, it's all right Alice. We all knew what would happen." Explains Nita.

"It's not all right. I dragged you all down, and now we're here."

They all sit quietly after my remark. Nobody makes eyes contact. I pull myself off the ground and join them by the cell door. I realize that we're all dressed in pure white clothes.

Past the cell door is a dark void. I can sense that there's way more to the room.

We stare for a few more minutes, and we hear a click of heels on the floor. It doesn't sound like Atrox. More like women's high heels, because the first tap is faint, before they lay down the ball of their foot. They walk with perfectly even strides.

I put the profile together in my mind. A woman wearing high heels. I feel a sense of satisfaction when I realize that I figured all that out by sound. But that doesn't answer my question. Who could it be?

Soon enough, the tapping gets closer, and it's accompanied by another set of shoes. Boots. Probably leather with thick soles. Still not Atrox. The boots probably contain large feet, and I can hear them sinking into the floor slightly more than the woman. The person is either really muscular, or slightly overweight.

I'm now itching to know who it is, and I'm answered as they come into view.

Conso, and Zed. The sounds match their descriptions. Conso is certainly a young, confident female, and Zed is a slightly chubby male. However, he doesn't look as chubby as he did when I first met him. He now appears slightly more muscular.

As we see their faces, Zane bangs against the bars, "Oh good, it's you guys. Can you help us out?" I'm sure he knows that the answer will be no.

Conso laughs—a wicked chuckle—and answers, "No. That won't be happening. We're here to simply inform you of the current situation."

She exaggerates clapping her hands, and lights turn on automatically. I'm practically blinded, because it's not just the lights. The entire room is pure white. Everything, ceiling to floor is white. Even the floor has built in light—probably to prevent shadows. It hurts my eyes to look at, but I feel fear growing within me. I know what will happen here.

"You all will slowly deteriorate in this room. Two things could happen. One, you slowly go insane. Or two, you become so scared, that you don't even want to eat."

Somehow, as she describes this, I feel like it's already happening. The thought makes me shudder.

"Conso and I will take care of you for a while. We'll make sure everything goes according to plan."

As Zed finishes speaking, a large white door opens slowly. A huge wheel spins on the surface of the door as it creaks open. The hinges groan.

When it finishes opening, I try to savor the color from the outside world. It's interrupted as President Atrox walks in, standing next to Eli.

My hand automatically bangs against the cell door. Why is Eli here? Are they keeping him captive too? Tears begin to flood my eyes, but I fight to hold them back. Something seems different about his presence. It's as though he's returned to the personality of the man I first met. I get the odd feeling that I shouldn't call him Eli anymore. He's returned to the wise loyalist of Pura, Oraculi.

When he sees me, he displays no emotion.

"Thank you for introducing them to the room." Atrox says, gesturing to Conso and Zed. Oraculi walks by his side briskly. Conso and Zed step back, and now all four of them stand in a line, just like us. The two teams stand face to face with each other, and I conveniently line up with Oraculi. He brings his hand up, as he blinks only one eye. He rubs the eyes shortly after. I almost get a feeling that it's supposed to be subtle sign. Perhaps the gesture is real, or he's trying to tell me something. It seems too convenient for him to wink at me during this moment. I'm hoping too much.

Before I can think about it anymore, Atrox locks eyes with me, "Firstly Alice," He begins to pull a few papers from his pocket, "I'm so glad that you finally know the truth."

I already know what the papers are. They're the medical records. It takes me only a few seconds to figure out how he got them. Oraculi.

Chapter 22

A SCREAM EXPLODES from my mouth. Why would Oraculi give him the records? He's putting himself in danger as well. It doesn't take me long to realize how Oraculi got the records in the first place. Oraculi gave Atrox the letters to prove his allegiance to Pura City. *He's betrayed me.*

It almost seems insignificant for Atrox to have the medical records at this point, but he can use every little piece of information he gets. He'll abuse the knowledge. I stare at the papers in his hands and notice my mother's letter as well. He has all of it.

The medical records alone won't matter as much, but if he has my mother's letter, then he knows what I know. Me finding out about M.C.

gave me leverage against him, and now I have nothing. But I'm still not sure how he got the letter. I certainly didn't give that to Oraculi. The thought makes me forgive him for a second, but I know that he still gave up the medical records. I find myself wanting to rip open the cell door, and slap Oraculi in the face. He's not the same person who so kindly helped me research M.C. He's not the same person who saved Amica and I from the soldiers in the student store. He's now a heartless minion, who does whatever Atrox wants. He's on Atrox's side now, and I have no effect on him. Perhaps he was never on my side and has been playing me this whole time. If that's true, then he knows where Amica is. He probably told Atrox, and now she'll die. I bang against the bars again, but none of them flinch. They're confused as to why I'm doing it for seemingly no reason.

"Anyways Alice, I would like you to know that these papers gave me a lot of information. I could never find anything about M.C., but Oraculi so kindly gave it to me. With his experience from the affiliate's program, he was able to find this information. Your mind will be harder to break down compared to the rest of the *Novus,* but it will break down. You'll go insane and fear your own shadow. These records helped Oraculi, and I tailor the process to fit your needs."

I clench my jaw while he speaks. Oraculi has betrayed me. He's carefully crafted a plan to torture me and manipulated me into trusting him. He did what Ordell was supposed to do in a better way. Now he's handed the plan over to Conso and Zed for them to execute it. I feel foolish for trusting him in the first place—my logic was blinded by feelings. If there ever were feelings. It's too hard to tell at this point.

Atrox and Oraculi exit the room shortly after, and we're left with Conso, and Zed. Somehow, it feels like Conso is almost as crazy as Atrox.

Conso glances to a soldier who's dressed in all white standing in the corner, "That's your caretaker and guard. He'll bring you food and water if it's allowed at the time."

I gulp at the thought. We might die of dehydration or hunger. I know this can't be. If we die, it will be at the hands of President Atrox. The soldier walks over to the cell door and unlocks it slowly. As he opens it, I almost plan to attack. But I don't. I'm not sure why, but I feel like something isn't right, "Before we begin, I would like you all to look to your left wrist," starts Conso. I shift my gaze towards my wrist and find a thick metal cuff occupying it. I'm not sure how I missed it before, "This cuff holds special technology we nicknamed Nightmare. It will be our main method."

Zed adds, "The Nightmare tech is capable of creating hallucinations. We've engineered them to deteriorate your minds quickly and efficiently."

Conso lifts her hand, and I notice that she holds a remote control, "This remote controls the cuff. The cuff controls your brain. Let's begin."

It seems so abrupt. She says let's begin, and I try to prepare for impact. But what will happen? I watch her closely as her finger moves to the only button on the remote. It happens as if it's in slow motion. Finally, her finger lightly grazes the button, and nothing happens. Although I don't back down yet. Something will happen. And I'm right. The white of the room slowly begins to blur together, until I'm left alone in a white void. I appear to stand on nothing, and everybody else has disappeared. The void is completely seamless, and I hear no noise at all. Slowly, a faint noise pries its way into my mind. It fades in, starting out quietly. At first, it's difficult to understand what the noise is, but soon enough I realize. A bomber plane. The noise grows until it's like a hurricane right on top of me. So, I run. There's nowhere to go, but I have experience with bombs. With no place to hide, the radiation will kill me at the very least. The noise of the plane remains above me, and I soon realize that it's following me. I can't escape it. I stop running, and crouch down low. It won't help me.

After what feels like hours, the first bomb finally drops. I can't see it, but the explosion shakes the void, and blurs my vision. More bombs follow it, and I'm left stumbling around blindly in a white void. I can't escape it. Too many visions come to me, most of which are from the previous war. But where are these bombs coming from? Who's dropping them? Bombs were outlawed after the last war, and if somebody uses them, then the colonies have rights to invade. So, who would do this? I'm not sure, but the piercing noise from the explosions leaves me feeling drained and I can't think anymore.

I stop running, and collapse onto the white floor. I'm left on the ground, and I do nothing. I can't do anything about it. The bombs are invisible to me, so I've given up. The bombs are growing louder and have reached a continuous stream of noise. A very subtle noise begins to echo within my mind. Soon, I recognize it as a laugh. At first, it brings me happy memories and peace, but I soon realize that it's a wicked chuckle. It grows louder, and the noise from the bombs slowly fades into silence. My ears are filled with the evil laugh, and the white void begins to change.

It fades back into the large white room. My ears are now fully focused on the laugh, and Conso reappears. I quickly realize that my face displays a look of horror, and that's what she's laughing at. She's laughing at my fear. I try switching my facial expression to be blank—trying to regain confidence—but I still feel scared from the bombs.

Soon enough, I begin realizing that the experience was fake. I vaguely remember Zed mentioning hallucinations, but the memory is too vague to be sure.

Zane is the first to talk after the experience, "What was that?" His voice is raspy.

Conso smirks, "That was your nightmare. Each time we use the remote, we'll program a different experience for you." She smiles sincerely, as if we should be excited for it. She presses the button once again, before finishing, "Here Zane, you can try again."

Immediately, Zane yelps in pain, and I know that the bombs have begun quicker this time. He tugs on his hair and manages to rip some out. Is this what I looked like during the experience? Nita runs over to him and screams, "Zane! It's just the remote, remember?" She tries to get his attention, but I remember my vision and my hearing disappearing in the void. The vision is present, and we can hear it. Nobody who lived through the war could possibly tolerate it. Nobody should have to tolerate it.

I run towards Conso, wishing I had a bit more power right now, "Stop!" I scream.

I can't bear to watch Zane squirming on the floor anymore, so I use the only power I have. Brute force. My hand grabs her arm, and I attempt wrestling her for the remote. She's stronger than I anticipated, and quickly rotates my arm behind my back. My body recoils, which only makes it worse. She finally releases me, and Zane stops screaming,

"I didn't even get to mention the other part of the torture. Fighting. We fight you, and it helps give you discipline until you can't even make your own decisions."

She orders me to the center of the large room, and I listen. My arm is still sore, but I can't afford to let her attack the Novus again, "If I win, then I activate the nightmare technology again."

I pause, thinking about what I want if I win. Obviously, I can't demand that we leave—it wouldn't really work. I can't really demand anything. If I win, then we're spared for the day, I suppose. As we get into position, I evaluate my chances of winning. We're both pretty tall, and similar in height. We also have the same thin build. Neither of our muscles are really developed, but if I was being picky, then Conso's are more defined.

The Novus stands quietly in the corner. I glance over, and notice Zane recovering. I have to win this fight. Before I can think anymore—and without any warning—Conso lunges at me.

I don't have time to prepare for impact, and she reaches me faster than expected. Her fist meets my stomach, and I wince. The blow takes my breath, and I have trouble regaining a steady pace. All I can do is brace myself for the next hit. The next hit is directed towards my knee, from her leg. Her style is quick and precise. She's been training. The hit throws me off balance, and I'm hunched over. I grit my teeth as she wrenches my head upwards. My teeth slam together, and I feel them shudder.

Her punch has helped me stand up though, so I utilize it by trying to throw a punch back to her. I realize how slow and untrained I am when she moves away with ease. We both step away from each other. She stares at me, and I decide to make the first move this time. I run and attempt to jump on her. I plan to bring her to the ground, but her leg kicks me directly in the stomach. I fall to the ground with a thump.

She reaches down and grabs my left arm. She begins twisting it, and somehow, I can't do anything about it. She continues twisting, and it will snap soon. The blows on my stomach feel painless compared to this.

Suddenly, Avetay yells, "Kick her!"

I realize that my legs are free, and silently scold myself for not realizing before. The opportunity is present, so I bring my leg up, and kick the back of her knee. Her leg collapses, and I manage to squirm free. I finally have the upper hand, so I jump onto her, pinning her down. She's lies on her back, and I realize that her hands are still free. Before I can do anything about it, she shoves her hands on my side, and I topple over. Now she's on top of me. She pins down my arms and legs, and leans in close to my face, "You lose."

Any remaining resistance leaves my body, and she gets up slowly. A tear floods my eye but falls back in since I'm still on my back.

My fellow Novus members rush towards me and help me stand. The room is silent. It's officially ended when Conso and Zed walk to the soldier in the corner, "Withhold food and water until tomorrow." Says Conso.

The soldier nods, obediently. Before they exit, Conso turns back to us, "Almost forgot. I said you would all get to have another nightmare."

Her finger taps the button, and the hallucination begins.

Chapter 23

IT'S BEEN THREE days since Conso defeated me. It felt like the biggest loss of my life. I haven't managed to look her in the eye since, because I've lost any confidence I had.

We sit in the white cell all day long, except for once a day. Every day, for a few hours, we leave the cell. We go into the white room, which isn't much of an escape. Inside the white room, we either fight, walk around, or do nothing at all.

I usually fight with Zane. I don't find it fun, but I found it humiliating to lose to Conso. I know it's made to ruin our minds quicker, but I don't care. I can't lose to Conso again. Today, we're let out of the cell, and I go straight to fighting with

Zane. Neither of us know what we're doing, but we're pretty evenly matched.

Zane and I line up in the center of the room, white rubber knives in hand. I hold mine upside down, and it's pointed towards him. We begin, and he runs to me quickly. His arm, holding the knife, shoots upwards, but I stop it with my knife. If it were real, the knife would cut his wrist. The only injury he gets is rubber burn.

My free hand manages to grab his knife, and I use both hands to twist it free. His grip loosens, and I now have both knives. I grip one in each hand, holding them directly in front of his face, "I win, again."

He walks away, embarrassed, while mocking me, *"I win, again."*

As he begins a walk around the bright room, Conso and Zed walk in together. Conso turns to Zed and asks," Zed? How long has it been since we've given them nightmares?"

He exaggerates a thinking face, "Probably a few days. That's a few too many."

Conso makes a disappointed face, "You're right. Let's fix that."

They both turn our way, and Conso holds up the remote. I've already tried breaking the bracelet. It's a thick metal cuff. I've found that there's nothing in this room that could possibly break it.

Just the sight of the remote makes me collapse. Conso mocks me. She laughs for what feels like hours—but is only seconds—before she yells for me to get up. I get up quickly, and notice that the remote has changed. Instead of one button, it has four. I presume that each button is for each Novus member. She teases us a few times by almost touching each button.

Finally, she sets her eyes on Avetay, "You first."

Avetay's face goes dark, but I can tell that she's trying to maintain confidence. I watch as Conso's finger touches the button, and Avetay falls to the floor screaming. Conso makes no effort to describe the hallucination, so I assume we'll all get the same one. It makes me wonder why they would need four separate buttons, and I realize that it's so we can all watch the horror.

I want to lunge at Conso and rip the remote from her hand. What made her this way? In the end though, I know it's thanks to Atrox. He probably manipulated her just like he did with Oraculi.

Conso presses the button again to stop, but Avetay still lies on the floor. We wait a few seconds, but she doesn't rise, "Get up!" Demands Conso.

Nita runs over to check her pulse, "The hallucination must have put her into a state of shock." Nita's words are precise. Perhaps she's the smartest of all of us.

Shock is a common problem nowadays. It's mostly thanks to the war, and most cases can't recover.

Conso sighs in fury and seems to search for something to break. But the room is empty. Instead, she just clenches her fists.

Conso orders the soldier to take Avetay to a hospital room. He carries her out quickly. I suppose they'll try to nurse her back to health, and then bring her back for more. It seems cruel to play with somebody's life, and hurt them, only to make them go through it again. Meanwhile, there are poor people who would kill for medicine in Pura.

Once she's gone, Conso begins pacing back and forth slowly, evaluating the remaining Novus members. She sets her eyes on Zane. Without much warning, Zane drops to the floor just like Avetay did. He screams louder than he did last time, and at one-point yells, "Don't take them all!"

This is a terrible method of torture, and I realize that there's only one way to escape it. We have to convince ourselves that it isn't real.

Conso presses the button again, and Zane stops screaming. He calms down, and I'm glad to see that he didn't go into shock. Now, Conso goes for Nita. She goes through the same process, and Nita screams. Nita's session seems to go faster than the others, and I'm relieved, until I realize that it's my turn now.

The Novus

I have no idea what the hallucination will be, but I know that it will be horrible. Inside my mind, I attempt to prepare myself by repeating a phrase. *It isn't real. It's just a hallucination. It isn't real.* But it will feel real. Whatever it is, it will feel real. My mind races as Conso glares towards me. Her deep blue eyes follow me, "You," she mutters.

She holds up the remote to make sure I can see it. Her eyes dart from me to the remote. I smile, to appear confident, but it fades as she presses the button. *It isn't real.*

I don't feel anything yet. She presses the button, but I don't scream. I don't run around the room from bombs, and I don't fall to the floor screaming. Instead, I stand there as though nothing's happening. I feel triumphant until I see Conso's face. She grins in a wicked way and disappears. No cloud of smoke consumes her, and no strange light occurs. She simply ceases to exist. After that, nothing happens for a few minutes. At least I think it's a few minutes. The white room seems to be impacting my mind.

Suddenly, whispers flood my head. They all say different things, but they generally mention, "*Alice, help us. Help me, please.*"

The voices can't possibly be real. I must be imagining it. *This isn't real.* The whispers grow louder, and a line of people appear before me. I recognize them all. Amica, my mother, my father, Auxillio, and even Tabitha. It seems odd to see them all here, and it's a seemingly random combination. Until I realize that these are the people I trust. They still whisper, and I can decipher what each individual says. All at once, the whispers shift. Instead of begging for help, they join into one unified voice and say, "Alice, you are alone. You're alone with nobody else."

The unified voice grows louder, and deeper, until it's a powerful force that practically blows me back with a puff of wind. I don't understand the situation at this point. Why would they say I'm alone when they're right here? As if they're answering my question, the voice says, *"We never cared about you. And you never cared about us. We trusted you, and you hurt us! How dare you!"*

The voice separates back into individual people, and I hear my mother say, "You killed me. It's thanks to you that I'm dead."

Amica repeats the same thing. The unified voice returns, and the line of people appears to be connected by some force. Something's off, but I just can't remember what, *"You will kill us all! Everybody will die because of you!"*

The final few words turn into a shaky scream, and they all break their positions. I'm still not sure what's happening, but they sprint towards me. It doesn't take them long to reach me, but I get the most overwhelming feeling when Amica grabs my shoulder.

I'm jolted back to reality, and the people are gone. The loud voice is gone, but the white room seems brighter. Light floods my eyes, and a headache jabs at my mind. Sickness fills my stomach and threatens to come out. My heart is beating faster than ever, and every breath I take is raspy, "I killed them all." The words escape my mouth in a scream, and I feel my mind drifting in many different directions. Is this what my mother meant? The Mutated Cerebrum condition is so fragile, that the smallest wound will kill it.

But this is not the smallest wound. I've finally admitted to myself the fact that I've killed people. I'm just as bad as Atrox. He killed millions of people he didn't know. I've killed those I loved. I can't deny that my case is worse than his, despite the numbers. My mind still examines the situation, and as the seconds drag on, it gets worse. I've killed Amica, and my mother. I've probably gotten Auxillio in trouble, and Tabitha is probably under investigation.

I faintly hear light shoes running towards me. I can't bring myself to look, but I know that it's Nita, "Alice, they're still alive. They're not actually dead."

Her words don't match with what I've seen. They are actually dead. Most of them at least. What is she talking about? I can't talk, but Conso does for me, "Nita, she didn't see the same thing as the rest of you. She got to see all the people she's killed."

I can sense Nita recoil at Conso's words, but she stays close. Does Nita think I've actually killed people? They wouldn't care for me anymore. I scold myself silently. Here I am, begging for attention. I've killed my mother, my friend, and now I'm trying to maintain a good reputation so my remaining friends—who I'm also slowly killing—still like me. I'm sick. There's no way around it at this point. I've hurt so many for my benefit. Even with Amica, I was protecting myself at the same time. I thought I was invincible because I was on the Magna Council, but I was too arrogant.

I glance at Conso, who appears to be bored. She probably doesn't want to fight because I'm too exhausted, and it's not worked into today's session. She sighs, before glancing to the guard in the corner, "Lock them back up."

We've sat in the cell for a long time. They haven't let us roam around in days, or weeks, or— I can't even remember. Perhaps they're doing this so we can reflect upon the nightmare. I certainly have. Sitting in the cell is a huge punishment, because it leaves us with nothing but our thoughts. The more I think, the more I feel myself decomposing.

Avetay returns a little after her hallucination. We all now sit in the cell quietly.

Only now do I realize that I was just asleep. My eyes are still closed, but I have the option to open them. I decide against it, as I regain hearing from the real world.

"They'll probably get in soon." I realize that they've been talking this whole time.

"It'll be another few weeks. It has to be."

"We don't know yet."

I finally open my eyes to question, "What's happening?"

They flinch at the sound of my voice, "Sorry, you've been asleep for a few hours." Apologizes Avetay.

Zane continues, "I was waiting for you to wake up. While you were asleep, the guard switched. There was a whole conversation that we could hardly hear, but I managed to hear the word *protesters*."

"We think that they're breaking in. Or at least preparing to."

I nod, as though I understand. They continue explaining what they think. Since the soldiers are switching, there must be some kind of patrol with shifts going on. Soldiers are limited, and the protesters probably came out of nowhere, so they had to improvise. This means that their defenses are weak right now.

While they talk, I seem to be the only one noticing the downside. If they break in, then there will be a huge loss of life. That's more deaths that fall under my name. It's my fault that they're doing this. The only advantage we have is that there's a greater number of protesters than soldiers.

"Alice, the citizens are becoming restless. They all want change. I just hope Atrox surrenders before—"

"He won't surrender," I cut her off, "He'll kill us all. Even when there's one person left."

Nita quietens, and I immediately feel bad for cutting her off. I sense that she's still scared of me from the other day, when Conso mentioned me killing people. Either way, my statement is true. Atrox would kill everybody without hesitation. He's done it before, in the war. Both him and his brother killed millions of people. It was an exaggerated quarrel between two brothers. A quarrel that killed millions of people and left half the world under rubble.

We stop talking about the protesters, but instead sit in silence. We all have given each other a space in the cell. I was given the back left corner. It is right next to a small air vent, so I get cool air streaming into the cell. Zane and Avetay sit against the bars of the cell. I notice them breaking out in sweat, and I begin noticing how hot the white room is. I examine the room and remember the light in the floors to stop shadows. All the light must be adding tons of heat to the floor.

I think about the protesters. How much have we missed? It's hard to decide when we've been locked up for so long and have lost all sense of time. Have they been fighting their way out of the protesting lot? Will they make it into the Pura building?

The other Novus members sit, heads pointed towards the ceiling. I suppose they're thinking about the same thing. My thoughts slowly shift from riots, to Amica. I feel bad, because I haven't thought about her in a while. It's like I'm not even honoring her death. Protesting was supposed to be my way of acknowledging her, but was it really? It was really about the Novus, and we hardly talked about Amica. We threw the story into the air and didn't claim it. Nobody did. Amica died without anybody knowing, and I'm the only one who cared. At least I care inside. To the outside world, it appears as though I'm only protecting myself. Aren't I? Am I helping everybody, or have I just protected myself? I would ask the Novus, but I fear their answer. I guess that's the answer though. If I know what they'd say—and I don't like it— then I am only protecting myself. I am a monster.

I wonder if Amica's currently walking through the wild, or if she's already found a colony. Maybe she never even escaped the city. It would take skill to leave undetected. And I'm not even factoring in

Oraculi probably telling Atrox where she went. I've really set Amica up for death. The odds are completely against her. Now I begin thinking about—for the first time—the radiation. I've never thought about it before, but perhaps the bombs left a lot. They never told us anything about it in school, because they didn't want us to leave. Although, if there was radiation, then they would tell us so we would be too scared to leave. The entire thought is confusing, and I push it aside.

Besides, thinking about Amica leads me to thinking about Oraculi. I can't bear to call him Eli anymore. It still shocks me every time I imagine it. How could he betray me? Somehow, it feels like I'm missing something. Or perhaps I'm trying to fill gaps that I'm hoping are there. I'm hoping way too much, for something that is probably nonexistent.

I try feeling the vent behind me. It currently brings in a steady stream of air, which helps to reduce the heat coming from the main room. My mind drifts, and I wonder what time it is. What day it is. What month it is—it's probably still the same month, yet it feels like it's been so many more.

I begin thinking about Atrox. What's he doing? Is he reminiscing his fun times with me, or trying to hold off violent riots? I'm not even sure if the riots are violent. They may have resumed back to the original protesting lot and become silent. Maybe, without a leader, they feel like they have no power. All I can hope for is that we win. If we do, then the Novus is freed and so is the rest of Pura City. It's also the only way that I can reconcile with the people I've killed.

My thoughts are interrupted by Conso walking in. I don't see her yet, but instead hear her boots. They get closer, and I urge my head to look up.

She stands silently. I notice that she has deep bags under her eyes, and her usually perfect blonde hair is knotted. She looks different without makeup, and her face is now so colorless. I try to guess what happened to her. Perhaps Atrox caught up with her little game. Or, she could have been helping Atrox decide what to do with the protesters. Changing from six people to two people is a huge change for a Magna member. She's taken on a massive workload, and it's showing. All this makes her seem a bit more human.

Her eyes meet mine, and she demands, "Today's session is another fight, Alice." She attempts to chuckle, but it comes out as a cough. I laugh at her pain until she holds up the remote as a threat. I silence myself immediately. I'm released from the cell, and we walk to the center of the bright room. I get the feeling that a fight isn't actually in today's plan. She must be stressed from the Magna, and she'll now take it out on me. I won't win this fight, but she won't either.

She says nothing, and immediately leaps towards me. Her fist is brought forward, and it connects to my jaw. I fall to the floor abruptly.

She hasn't grabbed me yet, so I retaliate by kicking her in the shin. A childish, yet effective move. She winces in pain, and I get off the ground. It takes a lot of effort to get up, but by the time I do, Conso grabs me from behind.

Her arms wrap around my stomach and throw me to the floor. I land with a thud and hear the other Novus members scream. I forgot they were watching.

She rolls me onto my stomach, and a few of my ribs land on the floor strangely. My arms are propped under my stomach, and Conso stands on my back. Her foot holds me to the floor, and I release a grimace of pain. She releases her foot to let me get up, but as I try, her foot draws back and slams me back down. My nose meets the floor.

She walks away slowly while yelling, "Get up!" Her scream is terrifying at this point, so I obey.

My bones creak, and I think I've broken a rib, "Conso, I give up, you—"

But she won't allow it. Before I can finish talking, she runs back to me, and grabs my arm. She spins it around and twists it. The maneuver was impressive and painful. She's pinned me to the ground in seconds.

It feels like she's constantly moving. She has me pinned for a second, and then rips me from the floor. She picks me up—as though I weigh nothing—and throws me a few feet across the floor. I catch a short break when she finally allows me to breathe. I evaluate my body and realize that I won't be able to get back up. My ribs are broken, my arm is dislocated, and I rolled my ankle on impact.

The Novus' voices are distant as they scream in pain—Conso must have activated the nightmare technology for them. I can't decide if Conso's fights, or the nightmares are worse.

Conso comes over and rolls me onto my back harshly. She sighs as she realizes that I can't move very well, "Fix her up. Quickly."

Her voice sounds agitated, and I wonder who she's talking to. I realize, when a few doctors dressed in white sprint towards me. I feel myself drifting into unconsciousness as they take me to an unfamiliar room. I have no time to examine it, because it seems like I fall asleep at once.

Chapter 24

I'M PARTIALLY AWARE as the doctors work on me. It feels as though I'm in between sleep and consciousness. Needles stab my arm, and surgical tools fill my ribs. The pain is excruciating, yet distant. Like it's in a different body, and I'm merely a spectator.

I slip into another deep sleep, and then wake up. I do this more times than I can count. Finally, I awaken and find myself in a different place. The room is white, and I wonder if I'm dead, until I realize that it's just the white room. I lie on the floor in the center.

My body immediately springs up—fearful of being kicked in the stomach. Lying out in the open leaves me feeling vulnerable, and I hope that

Conso isn't around to see me. I rush to the cell where the rest of the Novus sits. They jump at the sight of me, but settle down as a guard lets me in.

It's strange how the cell is now a place of refuge. Last time I was in here, I was complaining about it. Now, it's the safest place from Conso. This leads me to think about yet again how much I've changed in this room. The best example I can think of is my test score. Is it lowering every second? Do I still have Mutated Cerebrum?

I sit in the same corner I did before, and the cool air from the vent soothes my back from the blazing hot room.

We stay in the cell for days. Conso and Zed haven't let us out, and they give us only water. No food. The food is typically rice—probably since it's white—but it's better than nothing.

Occasionally, we'll discuss the protesters, however we have no new information. The guards still switch, but they no longer speak to each other.

Technically, we've lost count of the number of days we've been trapped in this cell, but I think it's roughly four. We sit silently as Conso, and Zed walk in. Zed holds a tray and tells the guards to release us.

The tray is a silver platter with a frosted glass cover.

Conso laughs as we leave the cell, practically tripping over each other. Zane gets up and begins to run towards Zed. Conso reflexively uses the remote. Zane falls to the floor and shakes uncontrollably. He stays there for a minute, before Conso releases him.

We stand in a line, drooling at the platter, "What we bring you isn't food," disappointment registers on my face while her words sink in, "But is in fact water." She dramatically rips the lid of the platter and raises it above Zed's head. She laughs at our disappointment. Sitting on the tray, are four small glasses of water. We all look to Conso in fury.

Zane is the first to move. He walks casually towards the water and grabs a cup off the platter. I know what he's about to do. So, I do the same. I walk to the platter and grab a glass.

We both now hold empty glasses, and Zane acts first. He brings the glass up and smashes it against Conso's arm. Blood is already spilling out, and I watch her rip a shard from her bicep as she screams. She grips the shard in her hand and swings it across Zane's face. It only cuts a tiny slit, but I watch him wince.

Zed still hasn't quite grasped the situation, so I make my move. My glass finds his wrist, and he shrieks while I rip the tray from his hand.

I bring the tray down on his head, and the remaining glasses fly off in the process. Zed grunts as the tray hits his head, and I notice a small wound open. I glance towards Zane, who is currently pulling out his own hair. Conso is using the remote.

Instinctively, I run to her—tray in hand—and slam it into her shoulder. Her body absorbs the blow, and it has almost no effect on her. However, she was still surprised, so I utilize that. My hand reaches for the remote and grabs it quickly. Before she can react, I press the only button and Zane stops screaming. My arm draws back, and I throw it across the large room. She's almost powerless now.

I still hold the metal platter, so I try to strike it onto her head. Except, she's too quick. She manages to stop it only inches above her head. Her hand releases her grip and connects to my stomach. I collapse.

Conso is about to deliver another blow, when Zane pulls her away. Avetay runs over and helps me stand. She scurries back to the side, as the fight becomes a confusing knot of limbs. My arms rotate in different directions while Zane and I team up against Conso. Zed stays to the side, and that's fine with me. I spin around as I hear somebody approaching. I assume it's Zed, so my arm rotates. As my fist almost connects to the target, I realize that it's not Zed. It's President Atrox. My fist stops inches from his face, and he demands, "Stop fighting."

We all stand intently, while Conso and Zed pull themselves together, "Sorry," Zed responds, "Sir."

He says *sir* firmly, and it sounds forced.

"That's all right Mr. Emberson. I'm here to see Ms. Harrington," he directs his attention to Conso, "It's come to my attention that you all have been fighting more than necessary."

Conso bows her head, and nods—as though she's sorry for her actions, "Sir, this fight was initiated by the captives."

Atrox holds up a dismissive hand and begins explaining to them the fighting aspect of the white room, "I thought I made it very clear, Ms. Harrington. The fighting was only for Alice, and only when it's on the schedule. Oraculi worked on the torture plan himself. He has extensive knowledge in this field, and you might have just ruined it."

"Sir, like I said, this fight wasn't started by me."

"But what about the last one? I saw the footage. You came in after a particularly stressful decision," while he says this, my thoughts from before are confirmed. The downsizing of the Magna Council has placed a great deal of stress upon the city, which seems odd, because the Magna used to only be one person. I suppose that learning to do it with many people makes you realize how small a role you actually play.

They continue arguing about the fighting, but Atrox wins. When they finish, they all leave. We're left to roam outside of the cell.

The Novus

Hours pass, and eventually we all relax by leaning upon the white walls. They've locked the cell door—so we can't get in—and Avetay leans against the exterior.

I begin to feel the effects of starvation. It's like a hole that slowly burns within my stomach. It also reminds me of the little girl from Malus town. We didn't always have lot of food in student housing anyways, but this is different. The combination of the white room, fighting, and now starvation buries itself deep into my mind. It feels like I'll die any second.

I'm just about to fall asleep when the steel wheel on the door begins to unravel. The door props open slowly, and the entire Novus stands.

The person who walks in is not Conso, or Zed, or even Atrox. It is a single soldier, holding a tray of food. The entire Novus runs towards him, but he immediately withholds the tray.

"Slow down guys, you'll all get some." I recognize the voice. It's the wisest voice I know. Oraculi. While the rest of the Novus begins to eat, I rip off his helmet, "What are you doing here?"

Before he gets the chance to respond, I lift my hand and glide it across his face. He winces in pain, but I don't care. He betrayed me. He deserves this. Yet, I get the feeling that he doesn't. "Alice, I can explain."

"You better be able to. How could you betray me and give Atrox the information about M.C.?"

My voice contains a lot of anger, yet his face looks sincere. I'm missing something, "I didn't give him the information!" His voice comes out as a yell. I've never heard him raise his voice before, but I'm glad that he's not actually angry. He sighs, before continuing, "Conso stole it from my house in the middle of the night." While he says this, I wonder if he's lying, but he can't be. I don't want him to be lying, "She was searching for it, and accidentally woke me up. I wasn't sure who it was, so I attacked, and she took me out. Then—"

I cut him off, "She forced you to give her the records."

It all pieces together in my mind. I remember that morning when I woke up and had the wound on my forehead. It was Conso. She must have been searching for the records, but I had just given them to Oraculi. The theory makes sense. It seems strange that she had access to memory loss technology, but I suppose that Atrox gave her whatever she needed. Then, I remember something else, "Wait, why are you here? You could get in serious trouble if you blow your cover!"

"There's only one security camera, and I told the security people to disable it for a private session. Besides, Atrox, Conso, and Zed are all… occupied."

"With what?"

"It's what I'm here to tell you about. The protests are becoming violent. Extremely violent. You guys only have one guard outside that door, and I am technically switching with the one that is usually inside the room." I wonder if it would be possible to break out right now, but I know we couldn't. We have to wait for the protesters. They'll break into the building, and then we'll escape when everybody's looking the other way. It feels satisfying to have a plan, but it doesn't change the fact that we're still trapped. We only have a little time before Conso's torturing breaks us down. If we go insane before the protesters break in, then there will be nobody left to claim victory. One of the government representatives would take Atrox's place, and we would be back to the same position.

Eli leaves shortly after we finish eating. He reminds us to act famished for the camera and slips out quickly. I'm glad to have someone to trust once again, but he feels too far away. It seems cruel, but I wish he or Amica was here in the room with me. They would be tortured as well, but we would last longer together.

We're left to lie around the main room, and we sit quietly. I do my best to act hungry for the camera, but it's difficult when I'm so excited.

Between the hope from Eli, and the food, my mind is sharper than ever—at least it feels that way, because it hasn't been sharp in so long. I'm thinking about Atrox's philosophy, and I understand it for the first time. He thrives on pain. *Pain is power, and power is pain.* The more I think about it, the deeper it gets.

I've finally discovered Atrox's key principle, and it's what I'll use to take him down.

Chapter 25

I FEEL AS though I've been asleep for only a few seconds, when my eyes jolt open. I'm not sure why, but I feel completely awake. I search the room and notice the other Novus members sound asleep. Something isn't right.

My eyes scan the room, searching for the source of my sudden awakening. They wander over to the cell, where I notice Conso lounging against the exterior. She stands inches away from Avetay. She seems to notice I'm awake, and begins, "I thought we could have a little talk while they sleep," her eyes meander around the room as she continues, "I've put them to sleep with the remote. They won't wake up until I command them to."

I gulp nervously, hoping to not find out why, "What would you like to talk about?"

She pretends to file her nails with the remote—as if she's bored, "I need answers. Something's going on that I'm not aware of," she points to the security camera in the corner, "I was looking at the footage from earlier when I was away. The camera turned off for a few minutes. Why?"

I laugh, before pushing further, "So now you want information from me?" my mouth curves into a grin.

Her chin raises, and her face remains unphased as Avetay suddenly bursts into a scream. Her eyes are closed as it begins, but they open abruptly. The scream rings in my ears as I realize why Conso is doing this, "Ready to cooperate now?"

I nod my head quickly. Avetay stops screaming and falls back into sleep. I try to think of a believable answer to her question. I can't give up Eli, or else our entire plan will crumble, "A soldier came in last night to give us food."

"Why would they disable the camera?"

I shrug, but she can't verify that my answer is false. It's mostly true, anyways, and she has no evidence that it's wrong. Her face displays a skeptical expression, but she moves on anyways, "Why won't Atrox kill you?"

The question surprises me. Of course, she wants me dead. But Atrox won't let her kill me.

She must be itching to get rid of us. She's had her fun, and now she's ready to walk away. Hopefully this means less fighting, although she might end up doing a fight and *accidentally* kill me. But would she? I'm still not fully aware of her position with Atrox and the government. Yes, she's on the Magna, but does she hold power in this space? She's conducting our torture but doesn't make decisions for it. Eli has done that for her, and according to Atrox, she can't change it.

I realize that I should be talking about the question. I'm not entirely sure of the answer, but I create the best one I can, "Remember those medical records Atrox had? They were mine. I'm sure you saw them." The words of her stealing them almost slip out of my mouth. If they did, then she would find out about Eli.

She nods her head.

"He killed my mother instead of me. He's torturing me with everything he's got, and I guess that he'll kill me when he runs out of ideas. I'm not really sure, but he also might be trying to mold me into a weapon. My condition could easily help him with military strategy."

She sighs, before responding, "I know that's not the full story, but it's enough." With that, she exits the white room, and I'm left alone. I think about how maybe even Conso has a tiny bit of human left within her. She settled for enough and let us off easy. Although perhaps she's getting restless. She's tired of torturing us and would rather kill us. I go back to the spot I was in before and prop myself against the wall. I find myself unable to fall asleep due to Avetay's scream still ringing in my ears. So instead, I get up and walk around. The large interior supports the foundation of going crazy, not to mention seeing the color white all day. *How did I get here?* The thought pops into my head unexpectedly, and I begin to feel sorry for myself. I'm only eighteen years old, and I've been forced to run the city, make speeches, and have even been tortured. I casually leave out the part where I've killed everyone I trust. But I'm still not sure about that. Yes, I've put them in harm's way, but didn't their deaths come down to their own decisions? However, it's not like they had very much of a choice. Amica could either leave and die, or stay and die. But my mother could have killed me instead. She would never kill me, and I'll have to live with that for the rest of my life. Her sacrifice saved me, but killed her, and now I must embrace that burden. I want tears to come, but they don't. I know I can't feel sorry for myself. I have to stay strong.

As I walk along the walls of the room—careful to avoid the sleeping bodies—I return to my starting point and notice the rest of the Novus twitching. Their eyes all jolt open simultaneously, and I hold my breath—hoping Conso won't activate the pain. Thankfully, she doesn't, and the

Novus lifts themselves off the floor. We stay silent, and their faces convey the same confusion mine did a little while ago.

The door to the room opens before we can move, and I watch as two soldiers walk in. They carry a thin black box, and I soon realize that it's a television. We leave them alone as they unlock the cell and lean the television against the back wall. It's all very confusing. Why would they give us a television if they're taking away all color? Perhaps seeing the color will shock our eyes. Or maybe they just really need us to see something. Well, I know that it's not shocking my eyes because the television is black. It's beautiful to see a different color, and I can't help but stare intently. But why is it here? The soldiers exit the room, and we all make our way to the cell. We close the cell door ourselves—although we can't lock it—and lean against it so we can observe the screen.

It's beautiful.

We're all speechless while we observe the beauty of another color. If they intended to hurt us with it, then it's certainly backfiring right now. After ten simple minutes of observing it, Nita asks, "Why would they bring this here?"

We all shrug, and it turns on seconds later. It cuts straight to a collage of images, and it takes me a few seconds to sort them out. It looks like the protesters. I see the protesting lot, and the many people within it. Only, they aren't holding signs, or screaming chants. Instead, they're using their bare hands to fight the soldiers. I inspect each image quickly—fearful that they'll go away—and get a grasp of what's truly happening outside the Pura building. Another image shows them fighting against the fence surrounding the Pura building. They aren't just in the protesting lot. They've made it so far.

The next image I view is horrific. It displays a street covered in dead bodies. Soldiers and civilians are sprawled across the road, each one lying in a pool of their own blood. I recognize the street as the one adjacent to the protesting lot. The whole collage gives me the impression that soldiers aren't allowed to shoot through the fence yet. Only in the protesting lot.

I gasp as I see the final image. It's taken from the inside of the fence with the soldiers. A crowd of protesters bang against the bars and standing in the center is a girl. She's medium height, with black hair. I immediately recognize the silver eyes. The girl is Amica.

Chapter 26

AMICA IS AMICABLE—is what I always said to her. It was almost a joke between us.

Amica was always friendly—is friendly. I thought for sure she was dead. I'm relieved to see her alive, but am also worried—and angry. Why would she come back if she'll be killed?

I look to the other Novus members who sit next to me. Their faces display the same shock as mine. They didn't know Amica personally, but they all knew what happened to her. Or what they thought happened to her, "She's alive," whispers Avetay. I remember her sister Joelle who died because of Atrox. It makes me wonder if Avetay could be jealous.

"She is," I spin around at the voice. It's Eli, again, standing outside the cell, "She's leading the protesters."

"Eli, why would they bring the television in here?"

"They didn't. I did. I ordered a few guards to bring it in."

"Did they ask why? Does Conso know?" Asks Zane.

"The soldiers didn't ask why, and only Atrox knows," he sees us freeze, and continues, "Don't worry. Atrox trusts me with his life. He let me disable the security camera, because I'm the one who designed your torture. Anyways, the television will help prolong your sanity."

It all seems so convenient. How has he convinced Atrox of his loyal position? And how are the two most high scoring students rebellious? Perhaps the test isn't as accurate as they thought. I doubt one of Amica's conspiracy theories are true, but the test can't possibly be accurate. According to the test, Eli and I would be criminals. As well as Avetay, Zane, and Nita. But we're not. We're good, and the test picked up on that.

The wheels begin spinning in my head. The test *is* accurate. It's designed to choose the kindest—and smartest—people for the Magna Council. We are. Atrox's idea of kind is enslaving people. He doesn't know that we're the real definition of kind. So, if this theory was correct, then technically all the Magna Council members are kind. This seems confusing, and it can't possibly be true. It would explain why the Magna Council is so alluring, but why are most of the members evil? The answer is the same as all my previous answers. President Atrox. He's scared everyone into following him. I suppose any evil Magna members were simply trying to stay alive. Besides, the test didn't pick out the brave. It picked out the smart, and kind. But it still doesn't add up with the slaves. I suppose the test has its own idea, almost as if it's living. Atrox molded it to fit his idea of good and bad, but the test is beyond him. The test is brilliant.

We all nod in thanks and turn around as the screen shifts. A middle-aged woman now occupies the screen, and she holds a microphone. She stands less than one-hundred feet away from the nearest protesters at the back of the crowd. I can't see the fights yet, because I assume they're near the front of the crowd.

"The riots are growing more violent as the days go by." She begins. I look to the corner where I see the date. It's been six weeks inside this room. I notice a single tear roll down Nita's cheek.

She's sad, but Zane snaps, "Well that's six weeks of my life I'll never get back." My thoughts turn from myself to the Novus as a whole. I can't quite tell how I'm doing in here, but it's obvious how the others are doing. Nita is breaking down—

she has a soft personality; I knew she'd be the first to go. Zane seems to be developing a worse attitude, and I can't quite decide if that's good or bad. Avetay seems to have remained the same, but I'm not sure how. She's relatively quiet, with an angst attitude.

The woman continues talking about the riots. Amica's picture flashes onto the screen, and she resumes, "This is Amica Lambert. She has been leading the protesters into violent riots. As we know from Alice Kingston's speech, these two are best friends."

She continues speaking, explaining the situation for those at home. Tears begin to flow as they display an aerial shot of the protesters. They zoom in on Amica. *Back down*—is all I can think. If she dies now, then all of this would have been for nothing. I know it's not true, but it feels like it is. For me, it's about saving Amica. For everybody else, it's about the test. I care about the test too, but this was all initiated by Amica. Without her, none of this would have happened. The thought gives me perspective on the situation, and only now do I realize how I've become a leader. My thoughts shift, and I now think *keep fighting*. I want her to fight all the way in. Once they're all here, we'll take out Atrox together. Then, all this will be over. No more slaves. No more suffering. No more President Atrox. I wonder what will happen afterwards, but I assume that the Novus might take over for a bit. But I will insist that Amica is added to it.

The screen goes black, and I sense Conso's presence, "Where did the television come from?"

"Two soldiers brought it in and turned it on. They said it was ordered by Oraculi." Responds Zane. I bite my lip really hard when he mentions Oraculi. He shouldn't have.

"Why? I didn't clear that."

"We don't know. Isn't that your job to figure out? We have no idea what's going on outside this room." As Zane finishes speaking, I realize that Eli disappeared. Where did he go? I'm still impressed about how he can disappear so smoothly.

Conso grips her remote, and Nita says, "Please don't do it again." She's begging, and tears are pouring quickly.

Conso smiles, and Zane adds, "Where's Zed?"

I'm glad to change the topic, and Conso's face tightens, "He wasn't cut out for this. He's a government slave now."

I can feel tension in the room after she says this. It's interrupted by Eli walking into the room. I smile at his presence.

He's no longer in a soldier disguise, but he walks in all on his own. Conso glares at him, "What are you doing here?"

She sounds annoyed, but his voice is smooth and calm, "Atrox sent me."

Conso looks at him with suspicion, and she asks, "Why did you give them the television?"

She examines him with her eyes, trying to detect any misstep to see if he's hiding something. He pulls her aside, and they whisper. I'm not sure what he says, but they walk back over and Conso appears to be embarrassed.

"Anyways, why did Atrox send you here?"

"I'm not sure, but he said that you would give me something to do."

She chuckles, probably because she's now in control of her former mentor. But then, she gets a small glimmer in her eyes. Not a kind glimmer, but an evil one, "I have a job for you," she begins, "You can try the remote."

He freezes. Anybody could see that he doesn't want to do it, but it goes deeper than that. If he doesn't, then Conso will know that something is wrong. She'll find out that Eli is against Pura City and throw him in here with us.

Eli straightens his face, and says in a cold tone, "Very well."

Conso smirks, as Eli plucks the remote from her hand. She watches him closely, scanning him for errors. If Eli doesn't do it, then our plan won't succeed.

He doesn't hesitate to point the remote towards Zane, but Conso quickly corrects him, "No," she gestures towards me, "Use it on Alice."

His expression deepens, but I can tell that he's trying to ignore his feelings. I know that there's no other option, so I have to endure the pain. My brain automatically repeats the phrase from last time. *This isn't real.*

My mind races, as he points the remote towards me. I know that he won't go easy on me—Conso wouldn't let him. All I can do is stay strong, although I'm not very good at it.

His finger taps the button on the remote, and the hallucination forms quickly. Everybody in the room disappears except for Eli. After fifteen seconds, Eli begins to change. He grows taller, and his face morphs into something else. Even the remote changes. I'm not sure what it's becoming yet, but I realize as it forms a handle. It's a gun.

I glance up from the gun, to see that Eli has become Ordell. He points the barrel of the gun directly towards me. Suddenly, another version of Ordell appears. He stands next to the original Ordell and points his gun. Slowly, more and more copies of Ordell multiply around me, until I'm surrounded. Every copy of Ordell points a gun towards my head, and I fear the moment when he'll shoot. I doubt that he'll miss like last time. *This isn't real.*

I dread the inevitable outcome of the situation and prepare myself to endure it. My thoughts are interrupted by gunshots going off. One by one, they explode, and the noise fills my ears. Although, once again, the bullets don't touch me. It shocks me, but I hardly even flinch—as though I expected this outcome. I know what will happen now. Each Ordell falls to the floor, and the pool of blood spreads. It grows, until there is a ring of blood encasing me. It seems to be rising higher and is now up to my ankles.

Finally—as I expected—Atrox steps into view. He points a gun directly towards me. His face contains a malicious expression, and the final shot goes off. I expect myself to crumple to the floor like Ordell, but instead, I find that Atrox has disappeared. Everybody who was in the room before has reappeared, and all my emotions escape at once. Sobs and screams escape my mouth, and it's the worst feeling I've ever had. How does Atrox kill so easily? He kills with no mercy and shows no sign of remorse. It makes me angry that people like that can exist, and I want to find him now. *I want to kill him.*

The thought creeps into my mind, and I begin to sob louder. When did I get this way? I used to be a poor student, trying to protect my best friend. Now, I've become a power-hungry leader, who wants to kill. I can sense Eli standing firmly in his spot, trying very hard to not move. I find myself wanting his comfort, but I know I don't deserve it. I deserve to run from Pura into the wild and die from dehydration. Like Amica was supposed to do, but instead, I forced her to become a leader. She didn't have much of a choice.

Everything I've done up to this point pours into my mind, and everything comes together. I've done more bad than good. I've manipulated, and even volunteered the Novus to be arrested.

My mother would look down upon me in shame. She would be disappointed in me, and so would my father. They would wish that they hadn't brought me to the Kansas refugee camp. I would have died in the final bombing, and the world would be a better place.

I cry for what feels like hours, but I know that they wouldn't stand there for that long. Then something unexpected happens. Eli breaks and runs up to me. He grips my hand before saying, "Alice, it's all right. I'm sorry, I had no choice."

But it won't matter now. He had no choice, and now he's undone it all. He could have either given us up or caused me pain. He's now unknowingly done both, but I know it's not his fault. He let his emotions blind him, like I did so many times. It's weird to see him make a mistake like this, but my mind doesn't linger on it for long.

My hand squeezes his tighter, and I can feel his hand going limp. He doesn't complain, and I'm not sure why I do it. It's not out of anger, but rather comfort. I need something to hold on to. Someone.

"I knew it," Conso says, angrily. She paces over to Eli, and grabs him by the collar of his shirt, "I knew that you were on her side."

She rips the remote from his hand and slaps it into his face with enormous strength. I'm snapped back into focus by this small action. I've watched her beat up the Novus, but I can't stop myself this time. I push open the still unlocked cell door and run to Conso. I draw back my hand and direct it to her nose.

The blow obviously surprised her, and even Eli. They didn't expect me to pick myself back up again, but anger boils within me. My hand repeatedly finds Conso's face, and she finally screams in rage.

When I throw another punch, her hand stops mine, and twists it. I can feel the exact moment when she shoves me to the floor. She screams something, and barks orders to the soldier in the corner. He runs over quickly and picks me up. He directs me towards Conso, who's only inches from my face when she says, "Your torture will be finished tomorrow." Her gaze shifts from mine to the rest of the Novus, "All of you will be finished tomorrow."

I watch everybody's reaction, and we're too scared to respond. We will all be gone tomorrow. Nita, Zane, Avetay, and I will all go insane. I'm not sure if she intended to end the torture so soon, but she has, and now there's no going back.

The Novus

She leaves the room shortly after, while the guard carries an unconscious Eli away. I didn't even see him fall unconscious. I worry as he carries him through the door. What will they do with him? Atrox won't allow him to die because of his expertise. Eli will probably talk his way out of it. *I was blinded by emotions. I still support Pura, sir, but I wanted to support a... friend.* I'm not sure why I paused before thinking about the word *friend*. Probably because I'm not even sure about what's happening between us at this point. Yes, he ran towards me when I was in pain, but wouldn't he do that for anybody? He's a kind and considerate person, so do I really think it's all for me? I'm once again being too arrogant and thinking too highly of myself.

The Novus stands silently, and nobody talks for the remainder of the day. I feel like we should be comforting each other, or at least planning. Instead, we sit silently in the locked cell.

The vent still sits behind my back, and I find that the fight has left my body. I thought that we could escape, but we can't now. It's too late. Amica will probably die, the Novus will go insane, and the protesters will break into the Pura building soon enough—probably in less than two days. They'll die too.

Chapter 27

THEY FEED US rice and give us water. We fall asleep shortly after, although I don't think any of us actually sleep. Even though we won't die, it feels like an execution. It feels like we're awaiting our death.

I think about my mother. She must have felt this way before she died. She sat in a cell, awaiting her death. Except hers was a real execution, and she was dying with purpose. I'm dying for nothing. I've done nothing.

When we wake up, they feed us nothing, and we sit in the cell quietly. We have no plan, and we don't know when Conso will arrive. I get the same feeling that my mother described. *I've accepted death.* I'll go insane today, and everything will be over. I fear that going insane will feel like a conscious death, but to be honest, I'm not sure what it will be like. If it is like a conscious death, then it might be the most horrible thing a human has endured. Although, I suppose death is conscious. Is it? I can't remember anything, or even think anymore. I'm too tired, and my mind is drained of all energy.

Perhaps it will be painful forever, and I'll feel the pain that Conso inflicted on me. Or maybe I won't know anything. It seems strange to know that I'll be a different person by the end of the day.

A few more hours pass—I think—and they give us a little more water. We're all subdued. The only distraction I have is Eli. What's happened to him at this point? If he didn't get his way with Atrox, then where is he? Maybe they'll put him in a white room like ours. Or perhaps they'll just kill him quickly. There's nobody important enough to oversee his death. Lapis and Alium have probably fallen out of the government by now, so they wouldn't do it.

If anything will save him, it's his knowledge. I'm thankful that he entered the Magna affiliate's program, because it makes him very high value to the city. Who knows if Atrox finds him expendable? Although, I didn't expect myself to be expendable considering my score. I suppose Atrox found me dangerous. Nobody had ever scored perfectly before, so he might not have known what to expect. This all supports my theory from earlier.

The test is accurate. It picks out the good people, and that completely backfired on Atrox because he had a different definition of good.

I just hope Eli's all right, and that some miracle will save him. And then he'll save us. Amica and him are our only chance. I'm hoping that the protesters will break into the building today. They have to reach it by tomorrow, or else they'll miss their chance. The soldiers would begin to shoot on sight. Amica has to know that.

My thoughts are pulled together, as I hear Conso walk through the door. I can hear her boots sink into the white floor. She's ready for the execution. It still bothers me to call it an execution though, because we won't die. But our souls will. *At eighteen years old, Alice Kingston will die. A mindless being will replace her.*

I look up and examine her. Conso's hair is pulled into a sleek ponytail, and she wears a dark blue pantsuit embroidered with the Pura flower. Her face is bright, and she smiles. She's way too excited. Weeks of her hard work will finally pay off.

In her hand, she holds the remote—it's become an object that we're scared of. It's what I fear most. Just the sight of it makes me want to run.

"Hello, guys!" Her voice is peppy, and it makes me despise her even more, "We need to get right to work. The soldiers will be given shooting orders, so I have other places to be."

Her words set my mind into motion. I put the information together and form a conclusion. The protesters will break in today. They have estimated that the protesters will break in today, and—since they haven't backed down—they'll start shooting on sight. It's exciting, because we might escape, but terrifying because so many of them will die.

All this makes me wonder about Conso's position in this mess. Does Atrox really need her help? I suppose that she's the only functioning Magna member remaining, but how much does she contribute with military strategy?

She commands for us to stand, and I notice a few soldiers standing around us, "Today marks the end of your sanity. I will be giving you the final hallucination, and it's the worst one yet."

She squints her eyes while inspecting us. I suppose she expected us to say something, but we don't have the energy. So, she continues, "I will begin in ten seconds. Any last words?"

Those words alone are tacky, but I suppose there's a reason for that. We're all silent, and even I can't think of anything. I wish I could have. The Novus deserves a better send off after all we've done. At least what the others have done. It should have been me who said the final words. But I didn't.

She nods her head, and then holds up the remote. *It's time.*

Chapter 28

I WATCH OUR bodies become stiff, and Conso smirks. She's already pressed the button, and I brace myself for whatever might happen. I'm still not sure what hallucination could possibly make us go insane.

Before it begins, I do my best to remember the phrase. *This isn't real. This isn't real.* However—like all the other times—I know that it will feel real.

Suddenly, Conso disappears. One by one, everybody else does the same, and I'm left alone in the white room. The white dims into black, but it's more like a shadow. It's like I'm surrounded by a shadow.

I focus on the darkness. *This isn't real.* Although it's dark, I can see my own body perfectly fine. It scares me to realize that I'm the only lit object within the darkness. The thought sends a shiver through my body.

Another object lights up about ten feet away. It's Amica. She stands silently, so I scream for her. She can't hear me. I scream louder as I realize that Atrox has brought her here to torture her, as he did to me.

This isn't real.

My voice strains while I yell, and it soon becomes hoarse. She still can't hear me. She sits quietly, and her silver eyes stare into my soul. My body tingles as I feel the presence of another person. Not Amica, but a person lurking in the shadows.

This isn't real.

I remain in my place and have now fallen silent in order to hide from the hidden person.

This isn't real.

Amica still stares at me. Finally, the creature reveals itself. It places a hand on my shoulder from behind me lightly. I try to run, but seem unable to move.

I'm not sure who the person is, but I learn that he's a man as he leans into my ear, and whispers in an echoing voice, *"You must kill her to escape, Alice."*

Before I can respond, he spins around, and is now in front of me. As I suspected, it's President Atrox. He wears a bright white suit—which reminds me of the white room.

The Novus

This isn't real.

He grins as he speaks once again, "*You need to kill her, Alice. It's the only way.*"

I attempt to respond, but can't, "*You've already killed her before. At least you thought so. What's the difference?*"

He continues to whisper things, and it echoes throughout the darkness. Atrox's voice isn't like it normally is. It's high pitched, like some kind of demon. Although Atrox is a demon all on his own.

Suddenly, I find myself able to move once again, and a knife materializes into my hand. I already know what he wants me to do. Killing Amica is the bridge between sanity and insanity. But it's a choice. Why would they make it a choice?

"*It's for your own good, Alice. You can't keep protecting her. Embrace yourself and the possibilities will be endless.*"

I'm now looking at Amica. She floats in the darkness, as if she's chained into her own shadow. Atrox is behind me. *This isn't real.* The thought is present, and I know it isn't real. So, if killing Amica is what gets me out of here, then I should do it. Shouldn't I? Is it the right thing to do? There's not another apparent option. I'll be stuck here forever if I don't kill her. For the next minute, I contemplate if it's worth it. I wouldn't actually be killing her because it's only a hallucination. A nightmare.

So it's decided. I remember that the protesters will break in today. I can't miss it, or else I'll never escape the white room. So, I begin to walk towards Amica. Atrox trails behind me slowly, and I reach Amica in seconds. A breath slithers through my nose and mouth.

I examine the knife. It's a long, eight-inch blade that's almost as metallic as Amica's eyes. The handle is blue wood, and it's stained with a glossy sheen. I know that I don't have much time left, before something else will happen. Perhaps Atrox would physically grab my wrist and force the knife into her heart. The thought disgusts me. Will I have to kill Amica? I'm still not sure entirely, but deep in my mind I know the true answer.

I raise the knife and grip it, so the blade points up. My hand grips the handle tightly, and it almost feels like it will snap in my hands. It feels natural. It's sad to think that the knife was made for the human hand. It's cruel. My mouth opens for my final words, but they don't come out. The hallucination isn't stopping me, but it's my own mind that does. Instead, I don't hesitate.

My hand curves up, and I know that the blade will meet her stomach. Only, I don't thrust it into Amica. At the last second, I spin around, and the blade penetrates Atrox's crisp white suit. It went in so easily—too easily, and I know that something is wrong. I didn't think this through.

My eyes dart up to Atrox's face, where it's been replaced with Amica's, "*The darkness can be confusing, Alice. It's easy to get lost.*"

The voice comes from behind me, and I spin around, leaving the knife in Amica's stomach. He tricked me, and I fell for it. Like all the other times, Atrox won. It was so easily laid out for me, but there was no way for me to win. I had to kill Amica.

My mouth releases a scream of fury towards Atrox, and my hands shoot towards his neck. *He's made me kill my friend. Now I have to kill him.*

The thought no longer disgusts me. I have to kill him, to end everything.

Just as my hands wrap around his neck, he vanishes, and I'm left alone in the darkness. Even though he's gone, he releases his final words, "*The darkness is the safest place to be.*"

His words echo repeatedly, and the shadows begin to morph into light as I fade back into reality. The brightness of the white room blinds my eyes, especially after being in the dark. It ends up giving me a headache, and my body falls to the floor while I try to fight the pain.

My eyes haven't adjusted to the light, and the result is a nauseating pain. I bury my head into the floor and cover my eyes with my hands. Now, I see darkness. An endless void, and it instantly relieves the pain. It feels much safer, somehow.

Atrox's last words ring within my ears, *the darkness is the safest place to be.* I realize that even though I've escaped the hallucination, I still have the choice. Will I embrace the darkness as he says? Am I really believing him? Do I have any reason not to? All these questions flow throughout my mind, and the answer doesn't reveal itself. Did I turn to the darkness because it was easier? It takes me a second to realize that I'm not just talking about now. I've turned towards the darkness many times. That's not my true place, and the test helped me realize that. If I face the darkness, then I become the darkness—just like Atrox. I've wanted to be the light for so long, but I've gone about it in the wrong ways. I have to face the light.

I struggle to move my head, but I do. It shifts from the comforts of my hands to the beaming white room. It still hurts, in fact, it burns, but it doesn't matter. It shouldn't matter. I have to stand up and own it.

Slowly, my eyes adjust to the surroundings. My eyes were squinting, and they open up fully now. As I scan the room, I see Conso. She stands quietly observing the Novus as they awaken. My eyes still ache.

Nita lies on the floor, and I watch her as she searches for the darkness. She covers her eyes with her hands and screams whenever a small bit of light enters her eyes. I run towards her first, "Nita!

It's alright, you didn't actually kill them!" I speak right into her ear, but she doesn't detect the noise.

My body shifts to Zane, who is doing the same as Nita. I turn to Avetay next, and as I suspected; she's doing the same. So why am I the only one who's okay?

"What is it going to take to break you?" begins Conso, "I've tried every method that they've created for this room, but nothing's worked."

I ignore her irritating voice, as I scramble around the Novus.

"Why won't Atrox just let me kill you!" She sees what I'm doing, and continues, "It won't work, Alice. This was the final test. They all saw a family member get killed. You killed somebody you love, because Oraculi engineered yours differently. Even after he betrayed us, Atrox kept him on board. He didn't even bother to get somebody who's qualified."

"Atrox kept Oraculi on board because he needed somebody to stick around who's not insane."

"Well, either way, it probably didn't work because of your," she pauses, before remembering, "Mutated Cerebrum."

My mouth forms a grin. This strange phenomenon has helped me for once. It gives me confidence, and I feel safer. But there's no way I could be immune to everything. I must remember that I'm not invincible. I've thought that before, and it was my biggest flaw. Now, I have to expose Conso's flaw, "It wasn't the Mutated Cerebrum. It didn't work because pain is your only weapon. Using it is your greatest flaw."

"I have no flaw!" she roars. Her face grows darker, "I will break you down, even if I have to do it with my bare hands."

I wince at the thought. She really thinks she's perfect. She looks as though she'll continue arguing, when the television within the cell turns back on, and our attention shifts. Why would it turn on now? Perhaps Eli *really* is okay and managed to turn it on from the outside again. Or Atrox turned it on to alert Conso. If that's the case, then something big is happening.

"All rioters have reached the fence surrounding the Pura building. We are guessing that they'll break in within a matter of hours."

The live video behind her displays the rioters pushing against the fence surrounding the Pura building. It sits under a pile of clouds. I notice that most of the rioter's clothes have been reduced to rags. Lots of them probably haven't gone home in a while. I search for Amica but can't seem to find her. Of course, there are thousands of rioters. *Please be alive.*

"Soldiers don't have orders to shoot yet like they did at the mass shooting near the protesting lot. However, it's estimated that they'll shoot very soon, if the rioters don't back down."

The Novus

I shudder at the thought. Soldiers shooting civilians with no restraint. No guideline. They will shoot willingly, to whomever they see fit.

Chapter 29

THE TELEVISION TURNS off, and I notice that Conso has disappeared. I suppose she's going to help President Atrox. That means I'm left here, with the newly insane Novus. I turn around to look at them. They all lay on the floor, still searching for darkness.

I suppose they'll search for darkness forever. How insane can you be, that you would rather find darkness than light. As insane as President Atrox I guess. I attempt to switch the perspective of my mind.

Alice Kingston creates speeches for Pura city, and then switches to opposing Pura. She protests and is now captured. Nobody knows where she is at this time.

The Novus

I hope that's not what people are thinking about me. I'd rather them love my intentions and know what I'm truly doing. My eyes shift back to the Novus, and I wonder what I should do now. I can't help them, so I have to listen to their screams.

But I can't settle for doing nothing. Not now. I have to escape before the rioters get in, and there's no better time than now. Conso's gone, and anybody else who's a threat is occupied. In fact, most of the soldiers will probably be outside as well. Their defenses will be down, and if I can escape, then I'll slip right past them. There's obviously no way to escape this room easily. However, they didn't specifically engineer this room for the smartest person in the city.

Since I can't escape, I attempt to turn the television back on. I've done it before, when the remote broke at my old student house. So, I walk to the television, and examine it. Eli didn't provide any exterior buttons, so I know I'll have to pry it open. It won't be difficult, because these televisions are made to be easily altered. Thankfully, my nails are very long—Conso didn't exactly give us the opportunity to cut them—so I dig them under the panel. Eli must have planned for this, because there aren't any screws holding it down. I easily rip it open, and I can instantly see the different electronic components.

This television is different than any I've ever seen, but it provides labels for easy access. I find the manual power switch in the top right corner and press it quickly. The screen displays a rainbow of colors, and then cuts to news coverage of the event. My face morphs into a smile, and I watch intently.

The first thing I see is soldiers preparing their guns. They load ammunition, and swap different parts. It also shows the opposing side of the fence, where rioters bang against it. I'm not sure how they'll break in, but I'm sure Amica's got it covered—otherwise, she wouldn't lead them here.

Anybody watching could easily see that the soldiers will shoot through the fence, while the rioters stand—helpless. I could only hope that they break down the fence quick enough.

Another possibility is that the soldiers are simply using the guns as a threat. Perhaps they're bluffing. But President Atrox wouldn't joke around. He has a list of tasks that he needs to deal with. Right below the rioters, is me. Which brings me back to escaping.

The large white room is sealed for sure, but perhaps I can find something to break it open with. I drift towards the cell door—which is made of metal—but realize that it's bolted in. *Obviously.* I'm denying all logic with hope. But, in all seriousness, I know there's not. I sigh in frustration and sit down.

I'm aware that I didn't try my hardest, but I honestly can't see any other way out. How did I think it would be possible to break out of a maximum-security prison? My mind slowly grasps the concept of giving up, and I walk to the other Novus members. Their cries have settled, but they still search for darkness.

I go to Nita first, "Nita." I whisper. I'm not sure why I whisper. Perhaps in an attempt to comfort her.

Her crying stops for a moment, and her head spins around. She appears to be blinded by the light, but she can't control herself. Her deep brown eyes lock onto mine, "He's coming. He's coming." Her voice is intense, and she grips my shoulders tightly. She's definitely scared of whoever *he* is, but I can't know without her telling me. She repeats the short phrase for about a minute, before she randomly screams, and returns to searching for darkness.

Who's coming? I wonder if somebody's actually coming, or if it's only in her head. Perhaps *he* is whoever killed her family member in the hallucination.

I decide to move on to Zane.

He seems to be tugging at his hair, while trying to hide from the light. I'm startled when the wheel on the door spins.

Without hesitation, I prepare for a fight. I run to the shelf in the room, where I grab the training rubber knives. They can't stab, but I could probably bruise with them. Nothing else is of use to me, so I need to run. I have to escape the second they open the door; it might be my only chance.

I perch myself directly in front of the door, just when the door begins to open more. I don't waste any time. My feet move on their own, and I'm already slipping through the thin crack. I catch a glimpse of two soldiers, but don't stop to examine them. I need to run.

As I run forward, I already hear them shouting for me to stop. They're obviously confused, but I need to run. They must be faster though, because I already feel their hands encasing my arms. They quickly restrict me and pull me back before I go any further.

Now that they hold me, I scan the hallway. The walls are made of light brown wood, so I can tell that we're very deep inside the Pura building. The floors are a tan tile, and the ceiling is only ten feet high.

I kick and thrash, but their grips are too tight, "Where are you taking me?"

They only give a brief answer, "President Atrox wants to use you." They drag me along. I realize quickly that my hands are free, and I know I can twist them out. There's a door down the end of the corridor. It has to be an exit.

Before they push me any further, I twist my arms free, and stab at them with the rubber knife. They recoil, and I take the opportunity to run. I've taken them by surprise, and it's the only advantage I have.

My feet propel forward, and I harness the energy I used when I was trying to find Amica a few weeks ago. I remember almost getting hit by the large truck.

As I run, I imagine that the men are the truck, and the door is the sidewalk. Even if I make it to the door, it's probably locked, and I won't have time to open it. I should have waited until they took me through the door to make my move.

I scold myself but run anyways. When I reach the door, I jiggle the handle, but it doesn't budge. Tears begin rolling, while I fumble for the knob. The soldier's footsteps echo behind me, and I scream while yanking on the door.

My body spins around, and I watch as the soldier's get closer. They stand less than ten feet away. *Nine. Eight. Seven.*

As I reach *six,* the door behind me gives in, and opens. I fall backwards onto the floor, and my head hits against a thick boot. My ears ring with gunshots. Two gunshots. I point my head up from the floor, and I see a tall man holding a gun. The light above casts a shadow over his face, and I can't tell who it is.

He reaches his arm down, and I latch onto it hastily. I'm thrusted from the floor in one fluid movement and brought to my feet. Less than five feet away are the soldiers lying on the ground.

They aren't dead, but their wounds are extreme. I wince as I watch them squirm on the ground.

Finally, I ignore them, and turn around. Behind me stands Eli. I can't help but smile as I run in for a hug. I cling to him like he's my source of life. He's saved me yet again. We hug for less than five seconds, when he releases me and I say, "I was hoping you'd find me."

He doesn't respond, but instead just grins. He no longer seems wise. He's sincere, and kind, instead of wise and rigid. I realize that's what I've needed all along.

He motions me forward, and we run. We run past the door, and we're brought into a slightly bigger hallway. We continue to run down the long hallway, and I wonder which door we'll take. I consider asking but realize that I trust him. I finally have somebody to trust.

He turns to the left and opens the final door. When he opens it, there's a staircase before us. Many flights spiral around, and I wonder how Conso did this almost every day. Unless if there's another way, of course.

Eli sighs in frustration, before he begins the long run. I follow shortly after. He's much faster on the stairs, and it puts a large gap between us. I hope there aren't any soldiers nearby.

As I run up the steps, Eli grows farther and farther away. He's almost reached the top when I still have halfway to go. He turns around now, and realizes how far behind I am. I suppose that he forgot not everybody is just below seven feet tall.

He begins to yell encouraging messages, but I block it out to focus. Although I soon realize that he's shouting something else, "Behind you! Run faster!"

He begins to come back down, and I glance behind me, where I see Conso sprinting up each flight of stairs. She grits her teeth while she forces herself forward. I'm nearing the top, when my vision goes dark. She's using the remote. I can feel my real body tipping over, and I tumble down the stairs.

Gunshots erupt, and I can tell that they're pointed at Conso, but they miss. The darkness begins to deepen, but I remember the phrase. *This isn't real.*

I can faintly make out Conso running towards me, and she shows no emotion in her eyes.

Eli's gunshots have stopped, and I wonder where he is. Thankfully, the darkness isn't a very bad hallucination, but I wonder how Conso customized a new one for this specific situation. Perhaps it's just a transition from an earlier hallucination. The remote is more complex than I imagined, and I realize that I've never really examined its features.

This isn't real.

Every step Conso takes makes my vision darker. A chorus of screams grow within me.

Where's Eli? I manage to glance up the staircase, but he's blocked by a railing. I hear a faint groan, and I think he's been shot.

This isn't real.

I pick myself up off the platform and manage to stand. I can see Conso, and I soon realize that she's shooting at me.

I dive up the staircase, and the railing blocks me. *This isn't real.* Every time I remember the phrase, it almost seems to lighten the darkness. It's as if a small portion of my brain remembers that it's only a hallucination.

My body is on full autopilot now, and I try ignoring the darkness. I stumble around as I try to climb up the stairs, but it's too dark. *This isn't real.*

The thought lingers in my mind, and it makes the darkness disappear for a fraction of a second. *This isn't real.* It lightens. *This isn't real.* My vision is almost fully back, and I can now move without stumbling. *This isn't real.*

I look up and manage to see Conso only one flight below me. Her face displays shock, "What are you doing?"

Her tone is angry, and the entire world seems to go completely silent. I need the perfect words to fill the air. I lock my eyes on hers, and respond, "It wasn't real."

Her face drains of all color, and she's left even paler than Atrox. My confident stare becomes a smirk, and before she can retaliate, I lunge for her.

The Novus

We stand on the same platform now, and I pin her against the concrete wall with all my strength. I draw her back and slam her into it again. She's still shocked by my recovery from the remote, and I utilize it.

But it isn't enough. How can I knock her out? I glimpse towards my wrist, where the metal cuff still wraps around it. She realizes what I'm doing, because I feel her struggling for the remote, dropping her gun in the process.

Before she can get it, I rip it out of her pocket, and throw it down the center of the staircase. It falls at least twenty flights, and I smirk as I hear the crunch on impact. Her face gets even paler, and I bring the metal cuff to her face. It smashes against her nose, but it takes a few more tries to knock her out.

When I'm done, it seems like that was too easy, but I can't waste time. I drop her to the floor, and she collapses. Then, I remember Eli.

"Eli!" I scream for him, and I hear him shout in pain. He must have been shot in a vital area for that much pain. He better not die.

Somehow, I manage to run up the stairs faster, and arrive at the top quickly. He's sprawled across the final flight of stairs.

"What happened?" I ask. His pants have a red hole in his calf, where he's been shot.

"Somebody shot me. I tried to come down for you, but I tripped and got stuck." He tries moving

287

again and cries out in pain. I begin crying myself. It's hard to see him this way. It'd be hard to see anybody this way.

I rip the long sleeve off my shirt and tie it around his calf, attempting to create a makeshift tourniquet. It only covers a small portion of the wound, but it's good enough for now.

His voice is raspy, but he manages to speak, "Alice, that won't work," I glare at him, remembering his extensive knowledge in this field, "Never mind, I'll work on it while I wait."

Any medical knowledge I have has slipped from my mind, and I end up instructing him to just apply pressure, "I'll try to drag you." I say, while wrapping my arms around his shoulders.

He laughs, "Alice, you can't drag me. You have to go. Find Atrox, and end all of this. It can't be the protesters who get him, it has to be you."

"No! I can't leave you now, somebody will find you and kill you."

"Nobody knows that I betrayed them yet. I'll be fine," I begin looking around, searching for another option, but his hands grab my face, and he focuses his eyes on mine. His deep eyes stare into my soul, and he's never looked more serious, "You have to go on your own."

It feels like we should say more, or do something else, but it ends. I run from him. While he applies pressure to his wound, I run to the president.

The Novus

While I run, I try pushing Eli from my mind. Although it's like he's made a permanent imprint on me, and I can't focus on anything else.

Chapter 30

AFTER THE STAIRCASE, I run into a hall that begins to look more like the Pura building. Luscious velvet carpets, beautiful tapestries, and golden tables all decorate the hall. I note that my eyes are still having trouble adjusting to anything that isn't white.

There are once again fake windows next to large doors.

As I run, I assess everything. Despite the weeks of torture I've endured, my body seems capable of running. I assume that the rioters are almost in the Pura building.

My face shifts into a grin, and I can't help but feel satisfied. We've almost won. I tell myself not to get excited, there's always a small chance that everything could change.

I wipe the thought from my mind to focus on running. I've made it to the end of the short hall and push open another large wooden door. On the other side is not what I expected. I'm already at the large marble hallway, although I notice subtle differences. When I look towards the huge windows, I notice a small logo in the corner. These are fake windows, which means that this isn't the real hall.

I run towards the large staircase at the end, and up the stairs quickly. I'm hoping that I don't find any soldiers. I should have taken the gun from Conso.

When I make it to the top of the steps, I open the large door, and find myself inside the main hall. I poke my head through and notice that it's clear. All the soldiers must be outside. As I run towards the next staircase, I hear gunfire outside. They must have just started shooting. I almost pause to cry, but I grit my teeth and keep moving.

I feel like I've run up many staircases, and my legs are growing more tired, but it's adrenaline that keeps me going. My feet find the top stair, and I step onto the platform of the second floor. The Presidential Hall. I can already see the president's office from here, and the Magna room on the side. *President Atrox is here.* The hall is extremely long, but that doesn't mean he's very far away. He's probably sitting in his desk, waiting for the outcome of the battle. He knows there's nothing else he can do. He can only wait and see if his soldiers come through. But even if they do, won't these protests all happen again? Probably not, considering who Atrox is. He'd probably make the law even more strict and enslave anybody who even makes a tiny motion of rebellion.

My chin lifts, and I take the first step. My body begins moving at a slow, but steady pace. As I walk, I think about what I'll say to him. It needs to be the greatest words in history. It needs to make up for all the pain he's caused. But I can't possibly represent the millions of people he's hurt. I've only experienced my situation, and I'm hardly aware of others.

I come upon the Magna Council door and decide to skip it. I don't want to get caught up with anybody in there. Instead, I continue walking forward. Towards Atrox. Towards the future.

No guards occupy the space in front of the office—I guess they were all put outside to hold off the rioters—so I walk right up to the door.

My hand finds its way to the knob, and I inhale. It's a long and deep breath, but it brings me a sense of peace. As I turn the knob and push, I exhale.

From the door, I can see Atrox standing on the balcony. He looks over the railing and into the setting sun. He doesn't know I'm here. Yet.

The Novus

As I begin walking forward, I'm interrupted by a single soldier—I suppose it's all he could spare. She pushes her gun right up to my face, "Stop right there, Ms. Kingston."

I shudder when the gun touches my forehead. My breathing is jagged, and I feel her flinch as my breathing switches, "Let her go, general." Says Atrox. The general sighs and releases her grip. But I still need a gun. My hand swiftly rips the gun from her hand, and I slam it into her head. She falls to the floor, unconscious. The entire motion is swift, and I don't think Atrox even notices, considering that his eyes peer into the distance.

With the gun in hand, I hide it behind my back, and walk forward slowly. When I reach the railing of the balcony—where I've given speeches—he doesn't even flinch. He says nothing. His eyes are fixed on the sky.

"It's quite a view," I begin. I fix my eyes on the sun, just like him. I find it interesting that the sun sets at the end of this battle. It's classic. So, I continue, "Too bad it's filled with dead bodies."

His bottom lip pulls back, as he performs a chuckle. We say nothing for a moment, but he finally continues, "I wanted nothing more than a perfect world. Surely you understand that Ms. Kingston."

His bottom lip springs back into place, and his face forms a natural shrug.

"But power takes its toll, and the result is pain. For everyone."

I wince at the term *everyone*. He feels no pain. No remorse. He feels joy in his endeavors. The thought makes me angry, so I snap, "You feel no pain. You heartlessly bombed the world and killed your own brother."

"Feeling pain, and inflicting pain are two different things," he begins. He's right. If anybody knows that it's me. I've unknowingly inflicted pain upon others, and received even more myself, "Killing my brother was the hardest thing I'd ever done. We never liked each other, but I certainly never wanted to kill him."

I know this is a lie. It has to be. Anybody watching the execution could have seen the pleasure he took in killing his brother. He ended the largest sibling feud in history with a smile.

We stay silent for a bit longer, and he says, "But nobody will let me make my case. They'll put me in the deepest dungeon they can find." The thought is strange. He's implying that they would be breaking the law. But there wouldn't be any law. It makes me wonder what happens after this. Perhaps one of the colonies will take the opportunity to destroy us while we're weak.

"There are always new beginnings," I explain—changing the topic, "They give us a second chance."

He smiles, and licks his lips awkwardly before responding, "I'm afraid it's too late for my second chance." His smile fades, and it becomes a shrug. I'm not sure how I can bear to stand here without shooting him. But I do.

I'm not sure if he's trying to coax pity. It's too hard to tell, and I'm not sure if he's lying. It's as if all the fire within him is gone. He's defeated, and he knows it.

"I've found that second chances are always deserved," I look at him. He turns his head towards mine, and his wrinkled eyes shine with a reflection of light, "But they shouldn't always be allowed."

The small sliver of hope within him vanishes until there's nothing left. It's not the happiest lesson, but it's the brutal truth. He's always given me the brutal truth, so it's only fair I do the same for him.

His eyes dart back to the sun, and he doesn't respond to me. So, I continue, "This all started because I wanted to save my friend. It's strange, but that's all there was to it. Now, it's become about saving the world," I pause for a moment, upset with my choice of words. So, I correct myself, "It's become about saving the world from you."

He says nothing. I expected a larger reaction, but it doesn't come. He just keeps his eyes fixated on the sun, and declares, "We'll be at odds as long as we live."

I nod my head in agreement. I look down for the first time, and notice that the number of rioters is shrinking. I panic, before realizing that they've gone inside the building. A smile crosses my face, and I hear the noise of people breaking in. They'll be here soon. I suppose they move slowly when there's so many of them.

Tears fill my eyes, and through blurry vision, I watch my hand point a gun towards the president.

Chapter 31

THE GUN POINTS directly to his heart, and it touches his suit. I can't seem to stop myself; it just happens, "I came here to speak with you. I wanted to make up for all the pain you've caused," I'm not sure if he hears my next words because they're masked with sobs, "But I can't make up for it. You have to die."

I don't shoot yet. I intended to say more, but the office door opens, and a girl walks through. My eyes are still blurry with tears, but I manage to wipe them away as she says, "Alice, don't do it."

Amica. I don't want her to see me this way. Isn't this what I'm trying to stop? No more killing. But I can't stop myself. My hand won't budge, and I'm not sure why.

Before I speak, I sob louder, "I can't stop."

Her silver eyes lock on mine. Those silver eyes always reminded me of our friendship, but it doesn't seem to matter right now, "We're all angry, trust me. But he doesn't need to die. He deserves to rot in a dungeon."

"He's my kill. If I don't do it now, then I'll live with the fear of him repeating all of this."

"If you do it now, then you'll live your life knowing that you've murdered somebody." She's chosen the word *murder* as a way to break into my mind, "Killing him is letting him off easy. He needs to live out his punishment," now Amica begins crying, "Alice, you don't want to kill somebody."

As she says this, I realize that her words are real. Too experienced. My hand almost moves, "What happened Amica?"

She collapses to the floor, "I thought it would help! But it doesn't, Alice. Killing doesn't clear your mind. It fills your mind with their screams."

I look to my friend. My best friend. My broken friend. My strong friend. This battle has hurt us both, and it needs to stop now. My hand moves, and the gun drops to the floor.

Atrox's body relaxes, and Amica slowly gets up, "Thank you, Alice," says Atrox. His voice is raspy, and I don't think he breathed that whole time. Neither did I. He continues, "But I've killed before, and I've found that it's the only way."

Atrox grabs me by the shoulder and points the gun against my back. Amica aims her own gun towards Atrox's face, "Don't kill her," pleads Amica. Her face is angry, "Or I'll shoot you."

"But Ms. Lambert, didn't we already establish that you don't like killing?" He chuckles as he says this, and Amica begins lowering her gun. It's up to me now. I can feel the cold metallic barrel through my shirt. I flinch while he clicks a bullet into the chamber.

"Please don't kill her. Why take another life?"

"If Alice dies, then I've gotten what I wanted from the beginning." He explains.

My throat is tight, but I speak anyways, "You never wanted me to die. You wanted to use me. But you couldn't, so you wanted to torture me instead." As I regurgitate his actions, Amica glares at me. She's warning me to be more careful, but I know how to handle him. I've done it before.

"You are correct there, Ms. Kingston. But I have no more use for you. If my city dies, then you're no longer needed." I feel his breath on my neck while he speaks. I wonder if I could spin around fast enough to dodge the bullet. He's older—probably sixty—and probably has no fighting experience.

Right as I'm about to move, he continues, "I would have killed you eventually, anyways. I'll have Conso killed as well for not breaking you."

"You have nobody to kill her. Your soldiers have all surrendered. We've won." Says Amica. I look to her from across the room, and smile. We've won. But it won't help me if I die now.

As Amica says this, I feel Atrox wince behind my back. I take the opportunity. My body spins to the side, and my hand wraps around the barrel of the gun as it vibrates with shots going off. My leg easily kicks out his knee, and he falls to the floor defenseless. Using the momentum from his fall, I rip the gun from his grasp and reposition it in my hand. I point the barrel at his leg—to make sure I won't kill him.

My mouth eases, and I allow myself to breathe. For the first time, I've beaten Atrox. And it's the final battle. The one that matters the most. A wave of satisfaction courses through me, and I hear Amica running towards me.

"Good job," She congratulates, "Where'd you learn that?" I don't respond. I breathe again, but not rapidly. It feels under control. Atrox lies on the ground silently—although his face is red with embarrassment. I think he just wants it to be over. He'd rather sit in a dungeon, then be shamed by his former citizens.

Minutes pass as I stand here holding the gun towards Atrox. Finally, two soldiers burst through the door. They glance towards Amica, and ask, "Is he in here, Ms. Lambert?"

The Novus

Amica nods, and gestures towards the floor. They rush over briskly and drag Atrox from the floor. I can tell that he pushes his weight downwards, because they have trouble lifting him even though he's thin. As I watch them drag him away, I wonder where they'll take him.

It's over. We've won. I can't stop thinking about this, because it doesn't seem real. It's strange to think that it's all over so quickly.

She releases me, and I send her downstairs to get the rioters out of the lobby. I need some space.

I walk towards the balcony, where rioters are already filing out of the building. They scream in joy, and some are even crying. More people gather, coming from their homes to see if we've really won.

An hour later, the streets are filled completely. This is probably the entire population of Pura City. I stay here, seated on the balcony for a bit longer, before going back inside. As much as I'd like to enjoy our victory, we currently have no government.

I walk to the former president's desk, where I sit down in the seat. On the desk sits a microphone, which I assume is for the intercom. The button is red, and I click it quickly. It turns green when I announce, "Could a few soldiers find Conso Harrington and Oraculi Sceptor? They are on the flights of stairs that lead to the dungeon.

Bring Oraculi to the Presidential Office and put Conso with Atrox."

My finger releases the button, and a muffled clicking noise comes over the speakers. I sit at the desk, patiently waiting, when the door finally opens. It's not Eli, but instead it's Amica once again, "I talked with a few people, and since you're the only remaining Novus member, you're the Interim President."

I nod my head. I'm not thrilled with it, but it's the only option we have for now. We now sit silently, waiting for Eli to come through the door.

The door finally opens, but it's still not Eli, it's a soldier. Not the same ones as last time, "Ms. Kingston, I sent two soldiers to search, but they didn't find Mr. Sceptor. Are you sure he's on the dungeon staircase?"

I nod my head, and tell him to get a search team, "Oraculi is…. High value to Pura. His skills will be needed if we're going to run the city." That's not necessarily true, but I don't care. We need to find him. As the soldier walks off, the only thing on my mind is hope for Eli to be alive. Not only did he save my life, but it feels like there's more to be done between us. I'm not quite ready to admit it yet, but I guess that means there's something to admit.

Chapter 32

IT'S BEEN TWO days since we overthrew the president. I've decided on the word *president* over *government*. Atrox was really the only bad one. Any others were simply looking out for themselves, and I can't blame them for that. I would have done the same if it weren't for Amica.

We've sent slaves into student housing until we find a better option. While the slaves are at the top of my list, I feel something else going on. Conso was never found, and neither was Eli. I worry for Eli, but I worry even more about a possible connection between the two disappearances. The thought makes my stomach churn.

Every day, I pretend to not think about the disappearances, but I do. Besides that, nothing has changed yet. How much could change in two days? Who knows how long it will take to rebuild the government?

However, rebuilding isn't my only task. With the slaves liberated, recovering the Novus is my top priority. Their condition has only gotten worse. It's only been a few days, but their brains have changed completely. We have our top scientists and doctors treating them, but they need to be brought back. If they don't recover, then Atrox has won in a small way. So has Conso. She's disappeared and hasn't turned up yet. I get the feeling that we'll find her soon, but it's too hard to tell. Perhaps she escaped Pura and forced Eli to go with her. I can't imagine her dragging Eli away, but perhaps she forced him with a gun. It seems unlikely considering his wound.

It feels strange to live in this new world. A world without the test, or even Atrox. I'm not yet sure if we can sustain it. Perhaps we'll have to fall back and rely on one of the colonies to take over. That would be the last resort, but a transition like this is huge. I can't deny that the test was efficient. It managed to organize the city into working categories, and each one contributed to Pura's growth. Enslavement should have never taken place.

The Novus

On my way to see the Novus—for another experiment—I wonder about how I could help their condition. I can't think of any possible way I could contribute, but there must be something. In their vision, they saw a family member die. All they need to do is see that they're still alive. But they won't accept it. Thanks to the hallucinations, they think that seeing their family member is fake. Everything to them is either fake or dead. That's how we've classified their level of insanity, and it's our only lead.

If Eli were here, then he could fix it. He engineered our torture, and probably created an escape route. I can't imagine he'd do it any other way. Unless if there isn't another way. I'm not sure, but he just might be the only one with enough knowledge to cure them.

I arrive at the hospital, where the Novus is recovering on the top floor. It's currently filled with patients from the riots—some bruised, some shot, and some dead. It now feels like our burden to honor those who sacrificed their own lives. Although, it's not much of a burden. It's a privilege. They saved us by paying the ultimate price. The thought is depressing. These people fought so hard for a perfect world but died trying. It was my greatest fear when Atrox was pointing the gun to my back. The only thought I had was, *what's the point of all this if I die?* But now I realize.

These people gave their lives for the city, and for the world. Their lives weren't worthless, because they became valuable the second they stepped onto the front lines. The thought is comforting. Kind of.

It's the only comforting thought I have. I now live inside an unknown city, where anything could happen.

As I push open the door to the recovery room, I realize that it was never about me. I was merely helping everybody else. Atrox used me to calm the people—which didn't work—and the people used me to overtake the government—which did work.

Now I stand here, helplessly trying to recover the Novus. As I watch the doctor desperately trying to get Nita's attention, she still mutters, "He's coming. He's coming."

And I still wonder who it is.

About the Author...

LINCOLN HARTLAUB is a teenage author who wrote his first book, The Novus, while uninspired during virtual learning. After over a year of writing and preparation, his first book is ready for purchase! Lincoln enjoys playing piano, doing Muay Thai, and utterly upending fictional character's lives.

I'd love to hear your honest opinion in an Amazon review!

Visit Lincoln's website!
www.LincolnHartlaub.com

END OF BOOK ONE